
BEYOND THAT LAST BLUE MOUNTAIN

MARGARET LIVINGSTONE

Beyond That Last Blue Mountain

HURST & BLACKETT

HURST & BLACKETT LIMITED
178-202 Great Portland Street, London, W.1.

AN IMPRINT OF THE  HUTCHINSON GROUP

London Melbourne Sydney
Auckland Bombay Toronto
Johannesburg New York

★

First published 1966

*This book has been set in Times New Roman,
printed in Great Britain on Antique Wove paper
by Cheltenham Press Ltd., Cheltenham, and
bound by Wm. Brendon & Son Ltd., Tiptree,
Essex.*

1

ROWENA FAIRFAX studied her left hand, and her mother
sighed as light glittered on the engagement ring.

'We haven't fixed a date yet,' Rowena was saying, 'but
it will probably be some time in the autumn. It all depends
on where we're going to live.'

'Of course,' Anne Fairfax murmured, and her daughter
gave her an uneasy glance. It had seemed so obvious that
when she and Keith Manning were married, they should
all live here in the tall, Pimlico house which had been home
for more than twenty years. Ordinary good manners had
decreed that the suggestion should come from Anne, but
Rowena had never dreamed that the idea might be un-
welcome.

Beside her on the couch, Keith waited as if he didn't
know what to say either, and for the first time, Rowena
gave serious thought to the fact that her mother had never
seemed to care very much for the fair and good-looking
young man who had been in and out of the house for
almost a year.

Anne's glance softened as she looked at her daughter.
Poor lamb, it was seldom that she found herself in a
position where meticulous planning and a study of the-
best-thing-for-everybody didn't work out to give her
exactly what she wanted. Rowena *looked* fragile, with her
smooth brown hair framing a fine-boned face, and wide
grey eyes which gazed on the world with seeming wonder
and a boundless trust. But there were times when thick

lashes hid the innocent wonder, when the delicate jaw firmed, and then people found themselves on the opposite side of the fence from where they meant to be, knowing only that they had gone there of their own free will – or had they?

A smile flitted across Anne's mouth as she met Rowena's reproachful look. It was easy to see that Rowena was only waiting for Keith to leave before starting in to change her mother's mind for her, and Anne thought, with some amusement, that this time it would be Rowena who would find herself in a position she didn't want to be in.

Defeat was far from Rowena's mind as she studied her mother with faint impatience. It was only common sense that the three of them should share this house which was far too big for one woman alone, but Mother had been surprised by the official announcement of the engagement, and would have to be cajoled into forgetting her pique and into acceptance of facts.

Rowena frowned thoughtfully as Anne crossed her lovely legs and talked to Keith about the benefits of travelling off-season for honeymoons or holidays. There was something odd about Mother to-day, a – a damped-down fire behind the gentian-blue eyes, and a dreaming curve to the generous mouth. And now she came to think of it, it wasn't only today. Mother had been gradually – well, coming alive ever since Father's death almost a year before, and it wasn't just a matter of adjusting to widowhood. After the first few months, the sober clothes and plain hairstyle had gone for ever. Now, Anne's dark brown hair was cut short, and the natural curls showed the truly lovely lines of head and neck. Blues and greens and singing yellows had taken the place of the blacks and navies and conservative greys which James Fairfax had thought most suitable for the wife of a solicitor and lay-preacher of long standing.

6

Rowena had noticed such outward changes with half-amused sympathy. After all, Mother was only forty now, and she had been just a shadow of James Fairfax for twenty-two years. Small wonder that she was tired of 'appearances,' and was tossing them overboard one by one. Only . . . wasn't it about time she stopped?

Keith stood up to leave, and Rowena looked with pleasure at his tall figure as he smiled at Anne. Good looks weren't everything, but when they were allied to ability, and to excellent prospects in the executive offices of a television company, well, a girl was entitled to feel that she had planned the future rather cleverly. And Keith wouldn't be a loser either. She was just the wife he needed, and, even more important, the wife he would appreciate.

'I think we gave her a bit of a shock,' he said to Rowena at the front door. 'She did manage a sort of "bless you, my children," but I doubt that her heart was in it!'

'It will be,' Rowena said briefly. 'How about your own mother? Are you sure she'll be pleased?'

'On the whole, she's delighted. But you know how it is – you're an only daughter, and I'm an only son, and as both our mothers are widows, I suppose they feel we're all they've got. If they were in the least bit alike, our marriage could draw them together to their mutual benefit, but I can't think of two people more certain to disagree!'

After he had gone, Rowena closed the door slowly, thinking about Mrs. Manning who was fifty-two, stiffly-corseted, cloaked in a dignified reserve, and whose pale eyes only showed warmth when her gaze was bent on her beloved son. She had been thirty when Keith was born, and sometimes it seemed that Mrs. Manning herself must have come into the world middle-aged and rapidly become elderly. No, the two mothers had no point of contact whatsoever, but it was a commentary on both of them that neither Keith nor Rowena had even considered living with Mrs. Manning after the marriage. Of course, the two-bedroom flat in Kilburn couldn't compare with the Georgian house in Pimlico, but even if the dwellings had been reversed, Rowena felt that neither she nor Keith would have been happy at the idea of sharing a home with his mother.

She returned to the drawing-room, allowing her gaze to rest with renewed satisfaction on the proportions which were so graceful a setting for the soft green and gold and white furnishings.

'It *is* charming,' Anne agreed, and looked at her, smiling. 'You made a lovely job of it. Which reminds me – how do you come to be home so early? Surely "Décor et Cie" hasn't run out of clients who want their homes torn to bits and replanned!'

'Not yet, but I doubt that I'll be there for much longer. It's been an interesting two years, but I'm having more and more rows with Daniel, and I can't do my best work in that kind of atmosphere. He and Denise have gone – well, "kooky" seems to be the nearest word, and they can't see that they need me as a sort of sheet anchor for their more conservative clients. I could leave tomorrow and take half their clients with me, but I'm not sure yet that I want to set up on my own. One has to have paperhangers and painters and all kinds of craftsmen to back one up, and I don't want to get too involved before the wedding.'

'The wedding,' Anne echoed as Rowena curled up in a corner of the sofa. 'You've no doubts, no hesitations at all? You're really going to marry Keith in the autumn?'

'You must have known months ago that I intended to marry him! Honestly, Mother, I can't see one thing that any woman could hold against him! You even said once that he reminded you of Father, and if ever there was an upright pillar of society—'

'Upright!' Anne exclaimed, and shot out of her chair as

8

if she just had to shake a burden off her shoulders. 'And narrow and cold and pitiless! How he loved his preaching engagements – he had so much head knowledge, so much advice for poor, suffering humanity, and not a spark of warmth in his heart to light up that St. Stephen face!'

'Why – Mother—' Rowena began, shaken by the passion with which Anne spoke and moved. 'I've never – you've never said anything like this before!'

'Maybe I shouldn't be saying it now either, but when I see you taking up with a man whose eyes remind me so much of your father's, what am I supposed to do? Stand aside and let you make the same mistake I made? There's an aura about people like that, and heaven knows I had long enough to become familiar with it. They have no *compassion*, no depths to their emotions, and they'll take your heart as their due and then put it aside somewhere and forget they ever asked for it!'

'Keith isn't like that! You can't *possibly* compare him with a man you don't seem to have cared about at all!'

'*Cared?*' Anne repeated, and gave a breathless sound like laughter although her eyes glittered with tears. 'I wish you'd seen me at eighteen! Wren Anne Stanwick, quite pretty but shy, suddenly pitchforked from a Highland manse to a secret operations unit near Portsmouth. That's where I met your father – Lieutenant James Fairfax was helping the chaplain by taking the weekly Bible class, and although I felt he was a bit "fire-and-brimstone" in his views, I thought he was wonderful.'

Anne stopped pacing for a moment and stared unsee-ingly at the telephone. 'Quite wonderful,' she said absently. 'I wasn't used to the – the language I heard on every side, I'd never seen a helpless drunk in my life, and I was shaken by other people's free and easy attitude to love-making. Some of the girls revelled in what they called their first taste of freedom, but I'd never wanted this

9

freedom, and I spent my first few months in Portsmouth being shocked to the core. I suppose this all sounds terribly naive to you?'

'No,' Rowena said thoughtfully, her expression one of absorbed interest. 'That village in Morven was dead long after the war, so it must have been stone age when you were growing up there. The few memories I have of Gran are of an old, old woman who could never have been very modern in her views. But go on – you've never told me any of this before.'

'It wasn't something I much wanted to remember. Well, I took refuge in church work in my free time, among the kind of people I knew, and it wasn't long before I saw that Lieutenant Fairfax was taking a great interest in Wren Stanwick from the unimpeachable background of a manse in the wilds. He certainly couldn't have had a more ardent disciple, and I remember thinking how right it was that the beauty of his face should match the beauty of his soul. To be honest, I was so much in love with the idea I had of him, that I never really gave any thought to his soul. I was eighteen, and he was in his late thirties, but we never once considered that the gap was too great. He was my kind of man, and my parents never mentioned the age difference either. You know yourself that he didn't look anything like sixty when he died – it's that beautiful bone structure that some lucky people have. You've got it too, and I don't suppose you'll ever look very much older than you do now.'

'That's nice,' Rowena said impatiently, 'but don't stop there. What happened to make you think he was cold and – and narrow and without compassion? If he waited till he was nearly forty before being swept off his feet, you must have caused a reaction somewhere inside him!'

Anne sat on the arm of a chair and looked at her with a wistful regret. 'Your generation *talks* about everything, but that doesn't mean you *know* it all. My mother may not have been modern, but she was very wise. She told me when I was about thirteen that the Almighty had given us our emotions and our feelings, that He had created us, male and female, in the way that seemed best to Him, and that it ill became us to be embarrassed by any part of the expression of love between man and wife.'

'That's rather sweet, and rather unexpected from someone like Gran. Why did you never tell me the same?'

'Oh, darling!' Anne laughed softly. '*You*, with all your knowledge and your textbooks, were the one who shied away from what you called "a cosy chat" – a horrible phrase which I would never have used anyway. You told me – with pained sorrow for my ignorance! – that you'd done a whole course on the subject at school, and that you'd probably forgotten more than I'd ever learned! I was furious inside that I couldn't make you listen to me instead of to those clinical spinsters in that wretched, fashionable establishment.'

'All jolly hockey sticks,' Rowena murmured, faint colour in her cheeks. 'I'm sorry, Mother. I'd forgotten how you disliked the place, and that I must have seemed quite a trial to you all those years.'

'Oh well, you were mad keen to go to boarding-school, and your father backed you up, so I just gave in. What *he* liked was the fact that the place was practically a nunnery, and that you wouldn't be mixing with boys until you were at least seventeen. You were a female, you see, and even if *you* were trustworthy, you were still a snare for the unwary male.'

Rowena sat up and stared at her. 'No! But he never said anything like that to me! Of course, I didn't see much of him while I was growing up, did I? I suppose by the time I left college and came home, he was so taken up with his retreats and preaching engagements that he forgot I was his! When did he start having ideas about women being a snare?'

'He was born with them,' Ann said bitterly. 'And they were nurtured by his parents who were repressed and narrow-minded and Victorian in the worst possible sense. Marriage was an honourable estate, and the arrival of children was the work of Providence, and it really appalled my mother-in-law that a woman should *enjoy* any of it! Anyway, my father came south and married us, and we'd managed to book for a few days at a lovely old inn near Lyndhurst. I'd got what I thought was my heart's desire, and that idea lasted exactly one day.'

She sat very still, remembering, and then she hugged herself as if she were cold and looked across at her daughter.

'It's nothing dreadful,' she said in an even voice, 'and I'm only telling you because it explains what happened a few months later when I fell in love with another man. My husband was shocked by my ardour. He expected a sacrificial lamb, and what he got was a partner who believed in the expression of love and delight and honest desire. It wasn't his *fault*, but I couldn't see that then. All I knew was that he had recoiled from me, as if I were a temptation from the Evil One, and that in his eyes I had fallen from the estate of "pure womanhood".'

'But it's not possible!' Rowena exclaimed. 'Men like that don't marry – they become monks or something—'

'My *dear* child, this didn't happen in the dark ages! Victorians and Edwardians of "good family" never mentioned what they considered to be the gross things of life to their children, and it's amazing how prejudice and narrowness weave their way from one generation to another.'

'Did – did you ever tell Father what your mother had taught you about it?'

Anne's mouth firmed and she looked away. 'That was when I despaired of the future altogether. He said it amounted to blasphemy, and he really believed it. The Almighty, he said, was concerned with our souls, not with our vile bodies.'

Rowena sat silent for a few moments and then shook her head. 'I don't see where you get any comparison at all with Keith. Nothing you've told me makes me think he's the least little bit like Father.'

'It wasn't meant to. We got on to this subject because you said I'd never cared about your father. Where I see the likeness is in their righteousness. They're armoured against all the pinpricks of conscience or tenderness or fellow-feeling that might make them deviate from their chosen path. I'm not saying they haven't got a conscience, but it's of the kind that only stirs when they've strayed from their own light. They're so *sure* of themselves and of their destiny, that anyone else's point of view has little value for them. Keith's outlook is a lot healthier than your father's was, and he'll probably be a very satisfactory husband in that way. But don't go digging for his soul, because you wouldn't care for it even if he had enough of one for you to find.'

'You're being very unfair,' Rowena protested. 'One unhappy experience doesn't make you a good judge of people, and what you call Keith's "assurance," I call his "stability." A girl wants a man who knows where he's going, who – who can be depended on to give her the kind of life she wants. And when they love each other as well, it seems like a pretty good bargain to me.'

'Of course, darling,' Anne agreed. 'As long as you're quite sure that Keith is the man you want to share your days with, then there's no more to be said. I've had so little to do with shaping your life, so little say in your education or your choice of a career, that I couldn't bear

13

the thought of saying nothing about this most important thing of all. You needn't wait till the autumn if you don't want to. I'll make over the house to you now, and you could even work from here if you decide to set up on your own.'

'From *here*? But – where will you be?'

Anne gave the telephone a haunted look and went to stand on the hearthrug. 'I don't know, yet. I've stayed in all day waiting for a message of some kind. If it's what I'm praying for, I'm off to Yugoslavia as soon as I can arrange it, and if – if it's all too late, I'll probably go anyway.'

'That other man,' Rowena said faintly. 'Over twenty years ago you fell in love with a *Yugoslav*? But who is he?'

'His name is Viktor, and that's the sum total of my knowledge of him.' She laughed shakily at Rowena's shocked expression. 'Oh, I did know that he wasn't married then, but anything can have happened in twenty-two years. He – he may not be alive any more, but I feel that somehow I should have known if he'd died. We were together for one afternoon – such a short time out of my whole life, so brief an event to have mattered so terribly all this time.'

She dragged her thoughts back from the past and looked at her daughter with compassion. Rowena was considering the situation and, by her expression, finding it unpalatable. In her view, the affair was too nebulous to count, and that her mother should step out of her settled, shadowy background to become a woman in love seemed utterly unreasonable. But then, Rowena was so like her father in some ways, cool, analytical, competent, emotions under control, and life neatly planned. She had loved her mother, yes, but she had never seemed to *need* her, and now she was upset because she had come up against a situation she couldn't control. It was untidy, and unnecessary, and odd, and the kind of thing that happened to other people but never to one's own.

Anne jumped as the telephone rang, and she went to sit on the arm of the sofa beside Rowena, and lifted the receiver. Rowena's eyebrows rose as she heard: 'Mrs. Anne Fairfax? This is Scotland Yard. Superintendent Stanley would like to speak to you.'

'Thank you,' Anne managed, and she smiled tremulously as she heard another voice a moment later. 'Anne? *Dear* Anne! It's been such a long time. I had your letter yesterday and I've been trying to arrange a meeting all day, but so many things cropped up that it's been quite impossible. I can call and see you now on my way home, or you can come here tomorrow morning at eleven o'clock.'

'Now, please,' Anne begged. 'As I've gone so far, I don't think I could bear another night of wondering. Allan – Captain Stanley – *do* you know anything about Viktor?'

He laughed softly. 'Allan will do – the Captain went back to the police twenty years ago. Yes, my dear, I know everything, and just to keep you going until I reach you, I may tell you that Viktor Petrović has never lost sight of you. He wrote to ask me about you at the end of the war, and we've kept in touch ever since, but I'll tell you everything shortly.'

Anne replaced the receiver and clasped her hands tightly. 'Petrović,' she murmured. 'So now I know his full name. I still don't know where he lives or what he does, and it doesn't matter at all. He remembered . . . and he kept in touch . . .'

Tears ran down her face like rain, and Rowena looked at her helplessly. This was something she had never seen before – Mother weeping in an abandonment of relief and thankfulness. In fact, she had never seen her mother cry

15

over anything, and if she had been asked, she would have said that Anne was the last person to find relief in tears.

She drew Anne to the sofa beside her, handed her a clean handkerchief, and tucked her arm within her own. 'All right,' she said practically. 'I'll put drinks on the tray in a minute, but let's not give the Superintendent a damp welcome. I had no idea you were on terms with Scotland Yard. I gather by the fact that you called him Captain Stanley that you had something to do with him during the war.'

'He was my boss,' Anne said after she had composed herself. 'We were a mixed lot in that unit – Army, Navy, Air Force and several hush-hush civilians. One of the things we did was final briefings for men who were to be dropped behind enemy lines all over Europe, and I'd been married about four months when Viktor came to us. When the Germans and Italians and Hungarians and everyone else invaded Yugoslavia, Viktor's army unit was caught near Skopje. Resistance was hopeless there and then, so they got out by way of Greece, and months later they ended up in Britain. It wasn't what they wanted, but there was no way back at that time, so they joined various allied forces and waited. When the guerillas got going under Mihailovitch and later under Tito, the allies decided to help them, and that was when the Yugoslavs over here were useful as liaison officers. Some were run ashore by the Navy in the Adriatic, and others were dropped by parachute. Viktor was going by air, and when he was all kitted out and briefed, we had an hour to wait before his plane left. We sat in a small, stuffy nissen hut, just the two of us, drinking coffee and feeding the stove with pinewood. That's why we've never had open fires anywhere we've lived – I couldn't have borne that sweet, aromatic scent of burning pine.'

Her voice died away, and Rowena got up to place a tray

16

of drinks on a low table. She was trying to come to grips with the realisation that her mother had regretted her marriage after only four months . . . that a few short hours should be enough to tell her that the man she should have married was a stranger . . . a foreigner who wasn't even a European but a Slav . . . that she had loved him through what must have seemed endless years, and at last had wept with joy just to know that he was still alive.

Rowena frowned absently as she polished a gleaming syphon, wondering how it would feel to lose Keith now and never to see him for twenty years. And not only that – to be tied to another man, and never to leave him because you were the kind of person who wouldn't break your vow to keep only to him as long as you both should live.

I haven't got that kind of faith, Rowena thought with a sudden desolate feeling. I'd either have got over being in love with this Viktor, or I'd have gone to him at the end of the war. And even then, I'd have had to be very sure of him. One afternoon – it's not enough to stake your life on. Maybe Mother's heading straight for a fall whatever she does now. To get to this man and to find she'd been only in love with a dream, or to find that he didn't care for her any more – that would be the death of more than an illusion. It would be the end of hope and faith, and of the mainspring that seems to have kept her going all this time.

A car drew up in the street outside, and Anne rose to go to the door. She smiled faintly at Rowena as she passed, but there was a tension about her that was new. Maybe she too had reached the stage of wondering whether dreams ever came true as they did in fairytales.

2

THE man who came into the room with his arm round Anne's shoulder was big and broad with grey wavy hair, and his smile was wide and contented.

'Wren Fairfax,' he was saying. 'You don't look a day older, and it really isn't fair! And I didn't remember that you were quite so beautiful either.'

'Morale-building speech, Wrens, for the use of,' Anne murmured. 'You're just as good at it as you ever were!'

She made the introductions and then shook her head as Rowena glanced towards the door.

'Stay with us, darling. You've heard most of the story anyway, and it may help to keep my feet on the ground if my twenty-one year old daughter is listening too!'

Allan Stanley put his drink on the table and covered Anne's clasped hands with his own as he sat by her on the sofa. 'We'll dispense with all finesse,' he said, 'and I'll tell you what I know. Viktor got in touch with me after the war, and I tracked you down and found that you were living here with your husband who was back in civilian life as a solicitor, and with your small daughter who was then about two. So that was that. But I knew what you meant to Viktor, and we used to write about once a year and exchange news. Last June, my wife and I toured Yugoslavia, and we spent a couple of days with Viktor and his nephew who were in the process of turning their old home into a hotel. Naturally, I checked on you before I left home, but there was no change in your circumstances, and all I could tell Viktor was that you were still living here with your husband and daughter.'

'June,' Anne murmured. 'My husband died in July. That was nine months ago. I – I'd had so many years of "keeping up appearances" that although I wanted to ask you about Viktor ages ago, it seemed only decent to wait until now.'

He smiled at her. 'I know. One reason you were so good at your job was that you were extra conscientious, and we always knew you gave everything you had to whatever you were engaged in. I – we never spoke of it at the time, but I've never forgotten how happy you were when you went off on leave to marry Lieutenant Fairfax.' He hesitated and glanced over at Rowena, and then seemed to decide that she might as well know this too. 'Then you came back, and oh, Anne, you were so quiet, so dimmed. I worried about you a lot, but you weren't the kind of person to discuss your private affairs, and you just sort of buried yourself in your work. I saw you light up again just once more—'

'The day Viktor came to us,' Anne broke in. 'I couldn't believe it was happening, and neither could he. Everything was so impossible. I was married, he was waiting to board a plane for Cairo and then for the Balkans, and it was the kind of mission he might not survive anyway. The war showed no signs of ending and – oh, the awful sense of minutes and seconds slipping away from us.'

'He gave you something to hold on to, though,' Allan said reminiscently. 'You were never again the lost, rather desolate waif who came back to us from leave. And what you didn't manage to learn about Yugoslavia after that, wasn't worth knowing!'

'It wasn't like a strange country to me. My uncle Oliver fought with the Serbs at Salonika in the First War, and he loved them like brothers and never stopped talking about them. He managed to tag on to one of the British Missions there in the Second War too, and I've been his best listener ever since! But I *felt* like a Yugoslav all through the war. I wept tears of rage and pity for their sufferings – tears they probably never thought to shed themselves. In my mind and heart, I was with Viktor and his friends in the woods and mountains. I felt I would *know* if anything happened to him – it would be like a light going out somewhere inside me.'

Rowena sat and listened with none of her inner confusion showing in her absorbed expression. All the time she had been growing up, Mother had had this other life at the back of her mind. Something to hold on to, Superintendent Stanley had said. All the time she had thought of Mother as a quiet, colourless, rather too obedient wife, there had been this 'light' which had beckoned and glowed and warmed the heart.

Allan drew some colour photographs from his wallet. 'I brought these with me today because I hoped I'd manage to see you. We took them last summer. You can keep that one of Viktor and his nephew – I'll get another print.'

Anne put the photograph on her knee because her fingers were shaking too much to hold it steady, and Rowena went over to sit on the arm of the sofa. The colours were true and brilliant – a cloudless sky, intense blue water, soaring dark grey mountains, a house of golden-white stone, and in the foreground two men, both dark-eyed but one with white hair and one with brown. Rowena gazed intently at the older man, trying to see what it was about him that had so captured a woman's allegiance.

He was big in every way, very bronzed, and his smile said that life was good, but to Rowena he was just another rather nice-looking man. The one beside him wasn't as tall, and he was slender and fine-drawn to a degree that spoke of previous hardship and privation. His smile was less pronounced, although there were laughter lines around his eyes, and his mouth was somehow sweet and gently curved.

'Viktor's gone white,' Anne said on a little gasp. 'I've never visualised him like that – his hair was a mass of thick, dark curls, with a few stray silver ones here and there.'

'He had enough to make him go white,' Allan said dryly. 'Some miles from his own house was the village where his sister lived with her four sons. Her husband was fighting with the guerillas, and on the day he was killed, Viktor got a few days leave to go to her. He'd joined up with the same group as his brother-in-law, and several men came from that area. About six of them made their way down from the mountains, and found the whole settlement non-existent. The ruling of the occupying troops in that part of eastern Bosnia was that for every German killed, one hundred Slavs would be killed, and as there had been a fight nearby between partisans and Germans, it was decided that the nearest Serbian community would pay the "penalty." So everyone was killed, men, women, and children, the houses set alight, and about a hundred people locked in the church which was then burned down.'

Rowena stared at him, and then at her mother who was shocked but not surprised.

'You say that as if it was the normal thing to have happened! As if it went on all the time!'

'It did,' Anne said flatly. 'The hatred of the Germans for the Serbs was of very long standing, and when they got the chance to annihilate them, believe me they took it. The Serbian nation *never* bowed to anyone, and that's one thing the German mind can't forgive. If you're conquered, you're supposed to stay that way, and the Serbs were loathed by Germans, Hungarians, Bulgarians,

21

and everyone else because they didn't know the meaning of the word surrender. We, in the West, owe more to them than you'll ever know.'

'I – I've never heard much about them. Even you haven't said anything, and you seem to know a lot.'

Anne gave her a level look. 'You wouldn't have listened, my dear. For your generation, the war is over and the way not to have another one is to forget everything we've ever learned, and just to *talk* about peace as if you were the only people who had ever wanted it. You don't approve of us older ones talking about wars that are past. I don't blame you, but it isn't the way to learn much about human nature.'

Allan nodded towards the photograph. 'They don't talk about it, but I don't see how they can ever forget it. When the men of the village were standing there, dazed and almost out of their minds, they heard a faint cry from a fir tree at the edge of the wood. It was young Simon Marković, Viktor's nephew, aged nine, and he was the sole survivor. He had been in trouble, and he'd gone to hide from his mother in that tree. He was there when the Germans came, and they never found him. He'd seen everything, and he was so rigid with fear and horror that it took two of the men to get him unclasped from the trunk of that tree. He had a bad time for months after, but he was tough, and he survived it somehow.'

Rowena looked again at the young man in the photograph, and her mouth went dry as she visualised herself clinging, stricken, to a tree while mother and three brothers and everyone familiar were done to death and set alight. But it was all a long time ago. People couldn't dwell on the past for ever. You built a new world for yourself, and you vowed that it would never happen again. It was evident from Simon Marković's features that he had learned how to put the memory of inhumanity behind him.

Anne suddenly gave a breathless little laugh. 'Here I am, wondering how soon I can get to Viktor, and I don't even know where he lives! Come on, Allan, tell me the rest.'

'I forgot you didn't know! Viktor's place is Srebro Kara, and the nearest airport is Cilipi which also serves Dubrovnik. You'll be going in the opposite direction, though, eastwards towards Montenegro. If you want to arrange for a hotel base, Igalo or Hercegnovi or Zelenika would suit you as well as any. You can always hire a car from there. Viktor's house is really beautiful and very old – built by a retired Dalmatian sea captain in the eighteenth century. It was getting a bit shabby, and as it was occupied by Albanian and Italian troops during the war, that didn't do it much good either. But they've done wonders with repairs and modernisation, and there's still room to expand if they decide to be a state hotel.'

'Won't it be his own place any more?' Rowena asked.

Allan shrugged. 'I think if you employ more than five people, you're a state enterprise. In that case, Viktor would be the manager, assisted by Simon, and the place would be run by a committee answerable to the local council or government or whatever. It seems to suit everyone that way, and Viktor never did bother much about personal possessions.'

'That's probably just as well,' Rowena said shortly. 'Mother, have you thought about the kind of country in which you hope you might spend the rest of your life? It may not be quite behind the Iron Curtain, but it *is* Communist, and not at all the life you've been used to.'

Anne smiled serenely. 'It doesn't worry me in the least. "Thy people shall be my people" is more than just a delightful quotation to me, and I'd love nothing better than to be one of them. Don't worry about me, darling. Your future's settled, and now that it is, I can go off with a quiet

23

mind. Your life was the only thing that was giving me cause for thought at all, and as long as you're happy about it, that's all that matters.'

'I must go,' Allan said as he stood up. 'I didn't tell my wife I might be late. Dear Anne, do come to me if there's anything at all you want to know about getting there, or if you want to hear any more about Srebro Kara. Are you going to write to Viktor, or just land on him unexpectedly?'

'Land there unannounced,' Anne said happily. 'I haven't any real *doubts*, but – well, I must see the look in Viktor's eyes when he sees me again after all these years. Bless you for coming, Allan. I had no idea when I wrote to you that you would know so much. I had visions of our trying to work out the best way of tracing a man who had disappeared into the middle of a war a long time ago.'

When Anne returned to the room after seeing Allan off, Rowena was sitting gazing into space, and there was a frown on her smooth brow.

'I want to come with you,' she said after a few minutes. 'I won't intrude, not at the beginning, but I'll want to see that you're all right – that you won't be having any regrets, I mean. I – I can't get used to the idea that you don't need looking after any more. I never thought of our being separated after I was married.'

Anne considered. 'Yes, do come if you feel you'd like to. I want you to meet Viktor too, and it might as well be right at the beginning. What will you do about your work? I want to get started as soon as I can make arrangements, and we'll need visas, and we should book accommodation as Allan suggested.'

'I'm on one job at the moment,' Rowena said thoughtfully. 'I'll finish that, which shouldn't take more than a week, and I won't take on any more. Daniel won't be heartbroken to see me go, and I won't be sorry either. Maybe two weeks will see us ready, visas, passports, hotel, journey, shopping. I can see we're going to have us quite a ball!'

Anne had always been a competent housekeeper – having had little else to occupy her mind and talents – and her arrangements for leaving home proceeded as smoothly as she expected. One afternoon she was studying the contents of her wardrobe, and thinking of the weight limitation on what she could take by air. Of course, Rowena could always send or bring things that had to be left behind, and somehow one didn't want to turn up loaded with baggage.

Rowena ran upstairs. 'Uncle Oliver's here.' she said impatiently. 'I'm expecting Keith at any minute, and you know how they love each other! Just because Keith was too young to be in the Army—'

'Send him up here,' Anne told her with a tranquil glance at the heaps of clothing everywhere. 'You might bring us some tea, dear, and he'll probably stay to dinner.'

'I'm sure he will,' Rowena muttered as she went out, and Anne smiled a little.

Poor Oliver – poor Rowena, they were separated by much more than the gap of age. Oliver's whole life had been the Army, and now that he was retired he dearly loved a listener. To Rowena, he was the 'Poona major' of fiction personified, a bore, an anachronism, and a dis-approver of modern youth.

'Here's a to-do,' he said as he seated himself on the chair Anne cleared for him. 'Why'd you never tell me about this Yugoslav chap all these years? I've lots of connections out there, and maybe I could have kept track of him for you.'

'I never told anyone, and you only know now because I couldn't disappear into the blue without telling you. What are you doing in town? I thought you were snugly settled in Gloucester with Cousin Hilda.'

25

Oliver's sturdy frame seemed to sag within his handsome tweeds, and his weatherbeaten face had more lines than before.

'She's a wasp,' he said unhappily. 'She buzzes, you know, and she feels undressed without a duster in one hand and a dollop of polish in the other. Can't be good for her, rushing around like she does, and she never stops talking either.'

Anne laughed softly. 'You mean you've got competition! But she's a good cook and housekeeper, and they're not easy to find. It's a nice little house, and at least your physical comforts are assured. You just can't settle down, can you?'

'I never did want to, I suppose. After seeing most of the world, there doesn't seem to be any particular place I want to go to alone. I miss the men I served with – they may not have been what Rowena would consider brilliant, but by heaven, they knew their jobs and they did them well. By the way, she tells me that young Manning is going with you too. Whose idea was that?'

'They thought of it together, and I don't mind. They'll be company for each other when I'm – I hope! – engaged elsewhere. Keith is taking two weeks of his annual holiday early, although I believe he doesn't altogether "approve" of Yugoslavia! Now then, don't *say* it! He has the idea that as the country is neither truly Communist nor truly democratic, then it must be merely opportunist and doesn't deserve a voice in the councils of the world! My dear, were we all as solemn and – and blind when we were twenty-two? Maybe we were. Anyway, Rowena is leaving her job, so they'll probably be out there for about a fortnight. I – I'm sort of taking it for granted that I won't be coming back myself! Talk about blind faith – I've never in all my life stepped out into the unknown like this, and if I stopped to think about it, I'd probably scare myself to death.'

Oliver thought it over for a moment. 'You'll be all right. You made a mistake when you chose James Fairfax – shouldn't think you'd do that again. Your father thought he was wonderful, but I never did. Spit an' image of a holy man I used to know in Peshawar, lived in a cave to keep away from the impurities of the world, and was bothered to death when they followed him in. About this Viktor Petrović – is he a Serb or a Montenegrin?'

'I've no idea. Does it make any difference?'

'Depends. Splendid soldiers, both of them, don't know the meaning of giving up.' He looked back down the years with a reminiscent smile. 'They got a bit mixed along the centuries anyway. The noble blood of the Lords of Serbia plus the mountain blood of Montenegrin shepherds made a splendid product of dignity and – well, guts. Be interested to hear what you think. You *will* keep in touch with me?'

Anne promised, and when he left that night she stood in the doorway and ached for his loneliness. Seen from behind, his bearing was so military, his step so firm and sure, and yet it must seem to him and to others that his usefulness was past, and that there was no place left for him in the modern world.

'What a *very* long evening,' Rowena said as she and Keith came out to the hall. 'Uncle Oliver thinks no one is worth anything if they haven't gone charging around Europe waving banners and lances, and yelling about freedom from tyranny!'

Anne halted and looked at the young faces before her, and the blue ice of her eyes sobered Rowena at once.

'If it hadn't been for Uncle Oliver and his kind,' Anne said, 'you would now be living in Nazi-occupied England. I don't think you would like it very much. And talking of waving banners – why are *you* able to do just that, to sprawl across highways, and to be a nuisance to the police?

27

I'll tell you why. Because you're living in a democracy, because all the Uncle Olivers of the past fifty years have kept your country free. For the first time in my life I'm beginning to wonder if it was worth it.'

'Wow!' Rowena muttered after Anne had swept past them and gone upstairs. 'That's the first time I've ever been sure she disliked my peace association activities. I knew she wasn't interested, but she never openly disapproved.'

'Nerves,' Keith suggested easily. 'She's taking off into the blue next week, and she can't possibly be sure that her reception will be everything she hopes for. Mother still can't believe she's really going.'

Mrs. Manning, Rowena thought later, had made that quite plain. It had been an uncomfortable evening altogether, and no wonder Anne had shied every time Mrs. Manning clasped her hands and tried hard to understand why 'a mother' should drop everything dear to her, and fly to a strange Communist country. To be a mother, according to Mrs. Manning, was almost to be sanctified, and although men were useful because one couldn't be a mother without them, it didn't make sense that one should think more of them than of a child. That the 'child' in question was a self-sufficient twenty-one made no difference to Mrs. Manning, and Rowena only got her off the subject by saying how wonderful it would be for her and Keith to have the Pimlico house after they were married. Then she wished she hadn't, because Mrs. Manning glanced thoughtfully round her sitting-room, and Rowena knew that she was thinking how wonderful it would be if she too were to end up in Pimlico.

Rowena mentioned the possibility to Anne that night on the way to bed, and Anne laughed lightly.

'I shouldn't worry, dear. Keith won't have her here at any price, so if you'll take my advice for once, don't say anything about it. Let him put her off in whatever way seems best to him, and then he'll never be able to tell himself that he did it all because you didn't want her.'

Rowena stared at her. 'Have you thought of the implications of what you've just said? She's his *mother* – she *lives* for him! If she wants to come here, and weeps all over Keith, *I'm* the one who will have to refuse to have her!'

'Why not wait and see?' Anne suggested. 'Keith is much too bright a young man to keep on being stifled by the excess mothering he's had all his life. He doesn't love her at all – honestly, darling, hadn't you noticed? He gives her what he feels is the respect and gratitude due to her, but sometimes I wonder if he even *likes* her much.'

'What's got into you lately?' Rowena asked crossly. 'You never used to make such sweeping statements, or to – to impute motives to people you don't really know very well!'

Anne slipped on a white lace and chiffon negligée she had just bought, and she smiled at Rowena's reflection in the mirror. 'No one ever listened to me before, no matter what I said! You and your father were very strong characters, you know! I've come to the conclusion that in the short time left to us I might as well tell you exactly what I think. You don't have to take any advice I may give you – as I said, you never did before!'

Rowena found that to have her mother saying exactly what she thought was a new and irritating experience, and she was glad when all their travelling arrangements were finally in order. The house now belonged entirely to Rowena, and she and Keith could hardly believe it when the business was rushed through, and Anne handed over the title deeds. In spite of the stars in her eyes, Anne had managed all her affairs with very little help from anyone, and on the morning they left, she patted the front door lightly as if saying goodbye to something she had never valued much.

They had all taken single air tickets – Anne, because she hoped she wouldn't be coming back at all, and the other two, because they intended to make it a real holiday and to return via the Adriatic and then overland across Europe.

A hotel car was waiting for them at Cilipi airport, and by dinner time they were in their rooms and wondering what the morning would bring. At the table that evening, Anne looked calm and serene, but when Rowena passed her the wine carafe, Anne's fingers were icy cold and she was sitting just a little too rigidly for comfort. Rowena smiled at her in a sudden surge of sympathetic under-standing, and Anne relaxed with a wry grimace for her own nervousness.

'We're taking a holiday unusually early,' Keith said as he glanced round at the busy scene in the dining-room, 'but we have special reasons for it. I wonder how so many other people have managed to get away now? They can't all be so wealthy that they don't have to work!'

'Many Germans are, these days,' Anne said. 'Yugo-slavia was always their favourite playground, long before the war, and it must have felt like coming home when they occupied the country in nineteen-forty. I see they're still here.'

Rowena sighed. 'The war's over, remember? Anyway, you can't possibly tell what country all these people have come from.'

'Like to bet on it?' Anne asked. 'We had to make special arrangements with our travel agent to get in here, because nearly all the bookings go to German agencies. Anyway, there's not much doubt about some of these people. Look at that man over by the pillar, the man with the red neck and the billowing wife – wouldn't you love to ask him what he was doing twenty-five years ago?'

'No, I would not! And I don't suppose he would care for what you were doing then either! It's all past, finished with, and it's time you stopped trying to make war on the Germans!'

Anne smiled faintly. 'Oh, *I* don't want to, but they have a nasty habit of dreaming of greatness they'll never have, and then they start pushing the world around to make their dreams come true. Must I approve of, and simply love everybody regardless of their funny little ways?'

'It would help,' Keith murmured. 'If you make a nation feel outcast and hated, you can't be surprised if they set out to show everyone how clever they are.'

'I see,' Anne said. 'You mean that if my generation and the ones before had loved the Germans, that nation would have automatically become civilised? It was really our fault that they indulged their tastes for death camps, and slave labour, and gas chambers? Well, it's certainly a new point of view! Ah, music from the vinery – enjoy yourselves, my children. I think I'll go to bed. It's been quite a day, and tomorrow – well, that may turn out to be quite a day too! Good night, my dears.'

She smiled at them, and left the dining-room, and Rowena half rose as if to go after her. Whatever happened the next day, tonight was the end of an era. She and her mother would be going their separate ways, and only now was she realising that the parting would leave a gap she could never quite fill. For a long time she had taken it for granted that Mother needed to be looked after, to have decisions made for her, to be told – in the nicest possible way – just what was what. Then she had first thought of Viktor as someone else who was going to take over the job of looking after Mother. But Mother hadn't needed any of them after all. She had had her own life of the mind and the imagination – well, perhaps she had needed

31

Viktor there in her mind, to keep her going – but her very presence had been a rock, firm and familiar in a changing world.

'She'll be all right,' Keith said as Rowena hesitated. 'It's tomorrow she might need you if any of her plans come unstuck. And if she does stay on, and this man is running a hotel, she'll have to watch what she says about "foreigners" who are bound to be among his clients!'

'She's not stupid!' Rowena flashed. 'I doubt that the word "foreigners" is even in her vocabulary! She was talking to *us*, about a certain nation, because she knows what we think, and she believes we're quite wrong. Well, she's had to listen to plenty from us in the past year, and from me for years before that, so you can't blame her for passing on *her* views even at this late date!'

Keith smiled and patted her hand. 'All right, darling – it's just that I'm not used to hearing her express herself so forcibly. Shall we go and see what the dancing's like? Or would you like to have an early night too?'

Rowena shook her head and followed him out to the vinery, sure in her own mind that Anne wasn't resting at all, but was thinking of all that the morning would bring.

Anne was kneeling at her bedroom window, gazing from the golden path of moonlight across the sea, to the dark soaring mountains which ringed the fiord on her left. It was a beautiful mild night, and after a few moments she looked beyond the peaks to one bright star high above.

'Please,' she whispered, 'whatever happens to me now, guide Rowena along the paths that will be right for her. And I don't mean let her be happy and never know sorrow or fear – but let her have a *satisfying* life – so that she'll find that to *give* love is more important than anything else.'

She stayed there for a long time, her eyes dreamy as she thought of Viktor a few miles away. Her breathing was

32

still inclined to be fast, and her hands were cold, but for good or ill she was committed to the greatest step of her life, and her eyes were serene even if her heart sometimes betrayed her.

The morning was bright and sunny, and she chose to wear a yellow wool dress and jacket. Keith and Rowena found her on the hotel terrace, and she turned to them with a wide smile.

'Isn't this a heavenly place? It's got everything – tropical palms and flowers here by the sea, and then those incredible black mountains over there. I can hardly wait to go exploring beyond them. Uncle Oliver said it was the wildest, most majestic country he'd ever seen in his life.'

'It is rather striking,' Rowena agreed. 'Nice suit, that. You look like a strayed sunbeam! We've arranged about a car. Keith has taken one for a fortnight, so we can get around a bit while you're – well, while you're doing whatever you'll be doing!'

When they left the hotel, the receptionist looked at them curiously when they mentioned Srebro Kara, and they were told it wouldn't be open for another month or so. Anne said something vague about having a look at the place, and went out to the car. She was interested in Hercegnovi which was yet to be explored, in the naval base at Zelenika, in the constantly changing scenery as they drove along by the sea, but all the time her mind was leaping forward round the next corner and over the next hill. And then, suddenly, there it was – the scene of the photograph which Allan Stanley had taken, and Rowena turned to give her mother a look of tense anxiety.

'It'll be all right, darling,' Anne murmured. 'Keith, please let me out here. You two can either park over there, off the road, or – or drive on, and maybe come back in an hour.'

Rowena got out with her. 'Good luck,' she said softly,

and kissed her, and then stood watching as her mother walked down the road towards the big old house of golden-white stone. Keith drove in to a natural lay-by on the same side of the road, and then he and Rowena walked slowly up the hillside to a flat rock where they sat down. Anne was walking slowly too, and Rowena glanced at a jetty opposite the house where several men were working around two boats in the water.

The utter stillness of one of them attracted Rowena's attention, and then he started walking up the road, stepping softly as if afraid to disperse an unbelievable mirage. Anne saw him at the same moment and stood still, and then they both started running until he caught her in his arms, and her hands went up with such tenderness to frame the face she had remembered so well.

Rowena saw another man detach himself from the group at the jetty, and, recognising him as Simon Marcović, she wondered what he was thinking about this turn in his Uncle's affairs. It wouldn't be surprising if he didn't like it at all. Then the lovely landscape blurred in front of her as her eyes filled with tears, and she felt lost, and lonely, and knew not why she should weep.

3

Keith placed an arm round Rowena's shoulder. 'It looks as if everything's all right, darling. This is no time for tears! I must admit that I was a bit doubtful about the whole thing, but of course I didn't have your mother's faith. Would you like to drive towards Kotor, or shall we just stay here and wait for whatever happens next?'

Rowena dried her eyes and watched as Anne and Viktor walked across the road and into the house. Simon Marcović hesitated at the end of the jetty, and then sat down on the edge of it and gazed at the shingle below his idly swinging feet.

'Let's wait here,' Rowena said, and managed a light laugh. 'Mother's bound to remember our existence before lunchtime! See that man sitting down there? That's Simon, the nephew I told you about. I wonder if Viktor ever told him about his lost love? Heavens, I hope he's got a nice nature – if he resents Mother's having come here, it could make things difficult for all of them.'

'Then it will be up to Viktor to decide which of them means the most to him,' Keith said easily. 'I've no patience with people who try to please everyone. They end up by pleasing no one, and making themselves miserable into the bargain.'

'But if you love people equally—'

'You can't. There's always someone in the world that you love more than you love anyone else. You may owe a *duty* to one more than to another, but it isn't always to the one you love best. I love *you* more than I love my mother or your mother, so your happiness will always come before my thought for them.'

'That's very nice for me,' Rowena said slowly, watching as Simon Marcović turned to the house, waved, and ran across to disappear inside. 'I hope you'll never find that you're being pulled two ways.'

He smiled, his blue eyes narrowed against the strong sunlight. 'I won't. I've got my priorities right! Now that the nephew's gone indoors, maybe we'll get a call at any time too. How long do you think we'll have to stay?'

'Aren't you curious about these men at all? No? Apart from the fact that it all concerns my mother, I'm longing to meet them both. They've had such a different life from ours – they've endured so much – I want to see what kind of people they've turned out to be at the end of it all. I like the look of that house too. Did you notice the carvings in the stone all round that huge front door?'

'Not really. Lovely view, though, and they've done a good job of matching the stone where they've built on those extra floors at the back. Ah, here comes young Marko-whatever-it-is. He doesn't *look* too upset, but Slavs are supposed to be on the inscrutable side, aren't they?'

'I wouldn't know,' Rowena said briefly as they rose and strolled down the hill. She couldn't expect Keith to feel the same anxious affection for Anne as she did herself, but his pose of the casual onlooker irritated her, and she was almost on the point of suggesting that he should return to their hotel and come back for them in the evening. But by then, Simon was near enough for her to recognise eagerness in his agile body, welcome in his smile, and a dancing light of happiness in his dark brown eyes. Her own anxious frown smoothed away, and her smile answered his as he came to a halt in front of them.

'I am Simon Marcović.' he said as he held out his hand. 'You are Miss Rowena Fairfax? And Mr. Manning? Please, will you come to the house? My uncle and his Anya – your pardon, I must say Anne! – they are not of this world at the moment! It was such a beautiful thing to happen. I never believed that it would come.'

Rowena put a hand on his arm, and he stopped and looked down at her. 'It's – it's all right then?' she asked. 'Viktor was hoping she might arrive some day?'

'He would have hoped for this until the end of his life,' Simon told her gravely, his eyes bright with understanding. 'You must come and see for yourself, and then you will know.'

Keith had walked on down to the road, and after a moment the other two followed him. Rowena's heart was suddenly light, because she knew already that Anne had been truly welcomed home. There was no longer any fear that 'the nephew' might resent her presence, and if his infectious joy was anything to go by, she was likely to take the place of the mother he had lost when he was nine.

The area between the front wall and the house was occupied by oleanders, palms, and lemon trees, but they were well to each side so that nothing interfered with the view of the great carved entrance. Rowena gazed with delight at the lively dolphins, the anchors, the tridents, and the bearded adventurer who had pride of place in the centre of the portal. The clarity and precision of the work had become a little smooth and blurred with the passing of two centuries, but the dolphins still flicked skittish tails in the stone waves, and laughter lines still showed on the face of the bearded sailor.

'*Very* effective,' Keith said. 'One would expect a thing like this to be preserved as a national monument.'

Simon smiled. 'There are so many of them! Craftsmen amused themselves long ago by carving even their stable doorways! One day we shall go round the fiord and show you many such houses in the different villages.'

'It's so – so gay,' Rowena said as her gaze travelled up the side of the portal and along the top. 'I suppose that's the sea captain who built the house? I'd love to have known him! The whole effect reminds me of the name of Lancelot's castle – the Joyous Gard.'

'The Joyous Gard,' Simon repeated. 'I like that. At Zagreb, I spent most of my time on modern languages and on our own literature, and often I have wished that I had given more of my mind to English writers.'

'Have you got a literature?' Keith asked in surprise, and then looked embarrassed. 'Sorry! I didn't mean that the way it sounded! One doesn't somehow think of this country as having had a literary history.'

Simon nodded towards the mountain range at the far end of the fiord. 'Over there, in Cetinje, was one of the earliest printing presses in Europe. That was in the fifteenth century, when Montenegro was a separate kingdom. Oh yes, we have our traditional poets and playwrights, even if they were not named Shakespeare!'

His dark eyes twinkled but Keith said nothing and waited for Rowena to go inside. The studded oak door was open, and she saw with some surprise that the hall floor was of marble worn smooth and creamy with age, and that the staircase was of wrought-iron and gracefully curved alongside the stone steps. None of it fitted the picture she had drawn of a soldier's home in the back of beyond, which was being turned into a hotel.

Simon led them towards the rear of the house and into a room on the right. Rowena took little note of the place itself because her mother was standing by the glass doors with her hand in Viktor's, and Rowena gave her a quick smile before looking searchingly at the big man with the thick white hair. His fine dark eyes regarded her from under level brows, and she could feel the strength and warmth of his nature, the sheer magnetism of his personality. Heavens, no wonder Mother had never been able to forget him!

'Rowena,' he murmured, and bent to kiss her temple. 'I am so happy to welcome you to my home. You are very beautiful, but – forgive me! – not so beautiful as your mother! She has not changed at all, and here am I, grown old and grey.'

He smiled down at Anne, and saw that in her eyes he was all she had ever wanted, and more than she had dreamed possible. The love between them was so naked and so dazzling, that Rowena looked quickly away and saw that Keith was waiting in the background with Simon. They came forward as she looked round, and when introductions were over, she was surprised and amused to hear Keith address Viktor as 'sir.' It would be a natural reaction from many young men, but not from Keith who had been so sure that all Slavs were peasant nations rushed into the twentieth century before their time.

'There is no champagne in the cellar,' Simon said regretfully, and then smiled at his uncle. 'The Riesling perhaps?'

Viktor nodded. 'The good one, in the end rack. And ask Natalya to bring glasses and to come and be introduced.'

Rowena went out through the glass doors and saw that the paved courtyard which was roofed with vines was big enough to take about thirty tables. They were well spaced, with tubs of lemon and orange trees between, and on the far side behind a wrought-iron railing, two swans idled regally along a stream.

'They will get very fat,' Viktor prophesied as he came out with Anne. 'Guests will feed them, and every meal-time they will sail up here and stare until they are waited on. The donkeys will have to be kept out of sight altogether – have you ever seen a grown woman as she croons over an ass or a donkey?'

Rowena laughed. 'Yes! Mother and I are mad about them! Have you really got some of your own?'

'Five,' Viktor told her with resignation. 'They are in that field beyond the boundary wall, and Simon will show them to you later. But they *work* for their living, and here and now I refuse your request to keep the smallest one in the garden!'

Rowena and Keith strolled towards the rear, glancing in at the big kitchen which was just behind the sitting-room, and where the doorway had been widened to ease the passage of waiters with trays. A paved path skirted the side of the house, and between that and the stream was a stretch of grass about thirty feet wide and fifty feet long. The railing enclosed only the vinery, and out here the grassy bank overhung the sun-sparkled water, broken only at one point by a silvery willow. On the far side, the woodland was fairly dense with the variegated greens of palm, pine, and cypress, and these gradually heightened as they grew up the slopes of the hill some way beyond. A covered way joined the main building to the annexe of new bedrooms and bathrooms behind it, but there was also a side door which guests could use on their way to meals in the vinery.

'I like it very much,' Rowena said thoughtfully, as she and Keith stood by the willow and looked back the way they had come. 'With the tourist trade being such a huge part of the country's industry, I can see Srebro Kara becoming extremely popular.'

'It's not quite what I expected,' Keith admitted. 'I can "see" your mother here quite easily now, but I haven't been at all sure she would care for what she was letting herself in for. The nephew seems quite happy about it too.'

'Yes,' Rowena said, and added nothing more. To her, it

was an understatement. Simon Marković had been over-joyed and he hadn't minded showing it. She wasn't used to an atmosphere which was so electric with unashamed love and obvious affection, and she told herself that she wouldn't care to live with it, and that she could certainly never be part of it. But she knew instinctively that her mother would thrive on an enveloping love such as she had longed for all her life. How strange that a mother and daughter should feel so differently about wearing the heart on the sleeve.

She looked up as Viktor waved from the door, and they walked back to be introduced to Natalya who was the housekeeper, and whose family were old friends of Vik-tor's. Natalya was about twenty-six, with short dark hair and large brown eyes. Her complexion was smoothly olive, and she looked very attractive in her white overall.

Simon poured the wine into long-stemmed glasses, lifted his own when everyone had theirs, and said softly: 'To Anne and Viktor, and may they have a long and very happy life together.'

Rowena smiled at her mother as she raised her glass, and although she was happy at the way things had turned out, she still felt like an outsider watching from the side-lines. But Rowena was proud of being a realist, and while regretting that she couldn't 'let herself go in an orgy of sentiment,' she was conscious of a great relief in having Anne settled happily here in the back of beyond.

'When is it to be?' she asked practically. 'The wedding, I mean. Keith and I have just eleven days to go, so do you think everything could be arranged before then?'

Viktor frowned and then glanced at Anne. 'I have no idea. Are you here on the usual three-month visa, or did you tell our Embassy in London that you would be staying here for the rest of your life?'

'That would have been taking too much for granted,'

Anne said, faint colour tinging her cheeks. 'I had to – to find out what you thought about it first. I had to be sure that you wanted me to stay with you . . .'

'And you were not sure?' he asked softly, and took her hand in his. 'No, perhaps I would not have been sure either. But your faith brought you this far, and it has been enough. What papers have you brought with you?'

'Everything official I could lay hands on. Birth and marriage certificates, my husband's death certificate, bank book, bank statements, even my W.R.N.S. discharge and conduct papers!'

Viktor laughed. 'I think that should do! We will start this afternoon, and see what can be done about hurrying everything through "official channels." But eleven days – well, I am not at all sure that arrangements can be finished by then.' He turned to Rowena. 'It would not be possible for you to stay longer? I know nothing of your work, but if you were to explain to your employers . . .'

'There's no trouble there,' Rowena said. 'I've packed in the job I was doing, and I'm not tied down. But Keith has to be back in London in time, and we were planning to take a few days travelling home across Europe. I – I never thought there wouldn't be time to fit in the wedding too.'

'Don't worry about it, darling,' Anne told her. 'You only came to see me safely into Viktor's hands, and it won't be a big ceremony. I've got what I came for, and I want you and Keith to have a lovely holiday, and not to change any of your plans because of me. Honestly, darling, I'd be much happier if you kept to your original arrangements.'

'That is sensible,' Natalya approved, as Rowena gazed thoughtfully into space. 'I could attend the bride – if she wished it, of course – and my mother and my two sisters would be here to assist in many ways. And if Simon is put in charge of everything, it is a promise that all will go well!'

She smiled at him with an arch, rather appealing amusement, and when he grinned in reply, Rowena found herself looking from one to the other in speculation. So that was the way the wind blew. Maybe it wouldn't be too long before a second wedding followed the first.

'We'll have to leave it until we know something more definite,' Rowena said after a few moments, and then looked at her mother. 'I think Keith and I might as well get back to the hotel now. When shall we call for you? About ten?'

But Viktor and Natalya insisted that lunch was almost ready, and that three unexpected guests made no difference at all. Keith seemed quite willing to stay where he was, so Rowena acknowledged to herself that she had wanted to stay too. She hadn't wanted to make Keith hang around when he was so keen on swimming and sailing – it was part of his annual holiday after all – but if it hadn't been for him, she would never have thought of leaving Srebro Kara that day.

They ate in the vinery, discussing all that was still to be done before the hotel opened in a month's time, and Anne eagerly grabbed herself the job of sewing curtains for the new bedrooms.

'You are not marrying me to become Madame-the-hotel-keeper,' Viktor insisted. 'The number of the staff is all arranged, and the work is allotted . . .'

'Oh, but I must have something to do with it,' Anne pleaded. 'Some little part of the work beforehand must be mine, and I'm not going to be just a decoration afterwards either! You've no idea how much I'm looking forward to being part of all this, to giving time and thought to helping you make it work.'

'I think I do have an idea,' Viktor told her gravely, and the understanding in his voice brought a brief sparkle of tears to her eyes. He knew little of her life with James

43

Fairfax, but he knew her, and he realised that her life until then had been something of a desert. There was that in his voice and eyes which told her that he would see to it that from henceforth the desert should blossom like a rose.

He pushed his empty coffee cup away and stood up. 'There has been no time to see anything yet,' he said. 'Come with me, Anne, and I will show you the rest of the house before we attend to the documents you have brought.' He remembered the others, and paused. 'You will excuse us?' he murmured, and gripped Anne's elbow and disappeared with her into the house.

Keith stared after them, and then turned to Rowena with amusement, but she refused to share it with him and busied herself with the little brass coffee pot. She had just realised that her mother and the man she loved had only had about ten minutes alone together since their meeting, and that they had suddenly got to the stage where they couldn't stand company for another moment. It was doubtful that either of them would see much of the house that day. Once in each other's arms, they would forget everything but the miracle of being together at last. Anne was even ready to forget that her daughter might not be able to stay for the wedding. She would like her to be there, but it didn't matter any more.

Rowena shivered a little as an errant breeze swept through the vinery, and when she looked up she saw that Simon was watching her with compassion in his wide dark eyes. She didn't care to have her thoughts read quite so easily, and she rose eagerly when Natalya started to clear the table. The two girls washed dishes in the kitchen, Keith went to the car for the swimming gear, and Simon went back to the boat engine he had been working on in the morning. Rowena used one of the new empty bedrooms as a changing room, put on her towelling robe, and crossed the road to the shingle beach at one side of the jetty. Keith was already in the water, swimming strongly some way out, but Rowena floated and idled nearer to the shore with an occasional thoughtful glance towards the house.

At last, Viktor and Anne drove out in a jeep from the far side of the house, waved gaily, and sped off down the road.

'A jeep, for heaven's sake!' Keith exclaimed as he came back to the beach. 'I wonder if that's the family limousine? Oh well, they sure can get around. Here, spread your towel on this rock – it's fairly smooth. Pity there's no sand, but the tourists can always find some further along, and that water's wonderful. What would you like to do tomorrow? There's a lovely sandy beach below our hotel.'

Rowena lay face downwards with her head resting on her arms, listening to the faint metallic sound of Simon's tools as he worked on the boat fifty yards away.

'Perhaps we'd better stay there,' she agreed. 'We might end up feeling frightfully "de trop" if we came here too often. Anyway, I'm dying to get my hands on some of those unfinished rooms, and it's really none of my business!'

'Colours and furnishings, you mean? Oh no, don't get involved in any of it! You've got very firm ideas on interior decoration, and from the look of him, so has Viktor! It's time they got a move on, though, if they're to open in a month – you'd think there would be one or two people working on it today.'

'Mother's arrival rather disrupted things, I should imagine, but Natalya told me that most of it was done in the evenings and at week-ends. Evidently, all sorts of craftsmen roll along after their own work is finished. I'm going in now. Ten minutes of this sun is enough for the first day. Keith – let's just wait to hear if Mother has any news about the wedding, and then we'll get back to our own hotel for dinner. Viktor would probably prefer to bring her back alone anyway.'

45

Keith laughed lightly as he picked up their towels. 'I'm quite sure he would! You know, if you called her "Anne," all this might be easier to believe, but when I hear you say "Mother," I can't square it up with all this grand passion and romance!'

'She's only forty,' Rowena said in an even voice. 'Are you suggesting that she ought to be thinking about old age and her latter end instead of marriage?'

'Don't be cross, darling,' Keith said uncertainly. 'You weren't all that keen on the idea in the beginning.'

'I tried to reserve judgement, and now that I find she's going to be very happy here, I'm happy about it too. She hasn't had much romance in her life, and it's only lately I realised that she was really a very romantic person.'

Keith looked at her thoughtfully as they went along the path towards the annexe. 'You've always said you were a realist, but now I'm not at all sure of it. I wonder what moonlight over the Adriatic would do to you?'

'Wait and see,' she advised with a laughing glance. 'No girl is *that* much of a realist!'

After she was dressed again, she sat on the edge of the bed-frame and looked across the grass to the willow tree. The window was open, and she could hear the stream running over its smooth brown stones and out to sea. It was a very soothing sound, and she sighed a little, knowing that she would rather spend her time here than in the hotel some miles away. This project was going to be fun, there was so much to do before the first guests arrived, and it would be a matter of pride to everyone concerned that Srebro Kara should be as perfect as possible at the start of its new life.

Perhaps it was the lovely old house itself which had charmed her. She didn't know. Perhaps it was the sudden realisation that her mother was almost lost to her for good, that they ought somehow to make the most of every flying moment now. Yugoslavia wasn't exactly next door to England, and when she and Keith were married with a family of their own, it wouldn't be easy to come even once a year. She knew very well that Keith wouldn't want to come, and you could hardly start out on married life with separate holidays or with disagreements about the destination. She had thought herself the last person to feel parting from her mother so much. Most girls left home when they got married, and many went to live abroad or even from one end of Britain to the other. It didn't make sense that she, of all people, should be casting backward looks at her mother.

I'm only just getting to know her, Rowena thought with a sudden pang as she rose and went to the window. I had an image of her in my mind when I was away at school and at college, and after I came home I never saw how false it was. Of course she's changed since Father died, but the essentials of her were always there, if I'd ever bothered to think she was worth listening to. She *could* have impressed herself and her opinions with more strength, but I knew everything, and what can a woman do with a daughter who shows her little but a kind of amused affection?

Rowena made an odd little sound of pain and self-derision, and went quickly out of the annexe. She had never really faced herself before, and the experience had been disturbing.

When the jeep returned at last, Rowena walked up from the jetty with Simon and Keith, and she didn't know whether to be relieved or disappointed when Anne shrugged lightly.

'We think it will be about three weeks before we can have the ceremony,' Viktor told them, 'but we will have more definite news in a few days. At least we know that there is no point in making arrangements for a week or ten days from now.'

'No,' Rowena agreed thoughtfully. 'Oh well, I'll think about it later. We're going back to our hotel now, so will you bring Mother when she's ready to come?'

Viktor returned her smile. 'I will try to return her at a respectable hour! You are sure you will not stay also? We are most happy to have you here at any time at all.'

'I know, and thank you, but we feel like dancing and there's some sort of gala at our hotel this evening. You'll – you'll see plenty of us before we leave the country!'

When they were driving back, Rowena looked along a track which disappeared among the hills. 'I wonder where that leads to? There are some lovely woods over there – it might make a good walk some day when we're feeling extra energetic.'

'We can try it tomorrow. Or we could go to Dubrovnik? It's about thirty miles from here, and I've been told it's one place we must see. And I'd like to try out my driving on the Mount Lovčen serpentines! The guidebook says there are twenty-five hairpin bends up to the top, and that the view is quite fabulous.'

With an effort, Rowena roused herself from her abstraction, and made a show of being interested in what they would do with their next few days. She remembered the time earlier that morning when Keith had said that he had no patience with those who tried to please everyone, and that they always ended up by pleasing no one, and making themselves miserable into the bargain. She could see, all too clearly, that that was what was going to happen now. If Keith hadn't been with her, she would have been quite happy to spend her time at Srebro Kara, even with Simon and Natalya, if Anne and Viktor were absorbed in each other. But she also wanted Keith to enjoy the only foreign trip he would have that year, and she was grateful to him for fitting in his plans with theirs. She loved him enough

48

to admit that there was no reason why he should want to spend his time with strangers in a half-finished hotel.

They enjoyed the gala dance that evening, and afterwards they strolled among the palms in the garden, and went to sit on the low wall overlooking the sea.

'No moonlight,' Keith murmured as he put an arm around her, 'but it's a very romantic spot all the same. Does milady approve of those huge stars, and the sound of small waves, and the scent of that juniper bush or whatever it is?'

Rowena half turned to lean back against him, and he held her closely. 'It's beautiful in every way, and milady approves! But when I say I'm a realist, it doesn't mean—'

'Never mind – tell me some other time.' He cupped her cheek with his hand and kissed her long and passionately. 'That's better. Sometimes, my love, I think we talk too much! Although we met at a peace rally debate, we don't have to carry it on in our private lives!'

'I know,' Rowena said, and kissed him lightly on the corner of his mouth, 'but it was wonderful meeting someone I could care about, and who thought as I did. I loved being part of the movement, but I didn't have anyone really *special* to discuss it all with. And then you came along, and – and we just sort of fused together at that first meeting.'

'It wasn't altogether from an intellectual point of view,' he reminded her with a soft laugh, and she smiled as she looked fondly at his fair hair and pleasantly-handsome features.

No, it hadn't been only his brains and his humanity she had fallen in love with. She was so lucky, she thought, to have found a man who had just about everything she could want.

When she got her bedroom key, she saw that Anne's was no longer on the board, and after leaving Keith with a linger-

49

ing good night, she knocked lightly on her mother's door.

'Well?' Anne asked eagerly before Rowena had time to say anything. 'I was dying to ask you what you thought about – well, about Viktor and everything, but we never had a moment!'

Rowena sat on the edge of the bed and kissed her mother's cheek. 'I thought he was quite gorgeous, and I'm not surprised you never managed to forget him! No, really, apart from his looks, I thought he was such a *nice* man. Silly little word, that, but you know what I mean – integrity, kindness, warmth. Darling, I'm sure you're going to be terribly happy together.'

'Why, Rowena . . .' Anne managed, and then groped under her pillow for a handkerchief. 'I'm sorry, but I never thought you'd approve quite so thoroughly! You've been very sweet about it all along, but I felt you didn't really care for the idea, and that you were just sort of putting a good face on it to – to please me.'

Rowena took a deep breath and gazed unseeingly at the single red rose on the bedside table. 'That's just what I was doing. I *am* sorry, Mother. I had no idea it was obvious to you that your hoity-toity daughter didn't quite approve of you! I took a long, cool look at the last few years when I was alone for a while today, and I can't say I was delighted with my memories. It shook me to realise that since I was eight, I only spent four months at home each year until I was nineteen. It all seemed very normal at the time – even the fact that a lot of the four months was taken up by school trips abroad! – and I loved boarding-school, but now it seems all wrong.'

'Not *all* wrong, darling. You've just said you loved it, and that's why I let it happen although I wanted you so badly myself. I felt then that if people were happy, that was all that mattered, but I don't believe it any more. Happiness isn't anybody's *right*. One ends up by choosing

50

what one regards as happiness, at the expense of self-discipline very often, and it has such a – such a flabby effect on one's life and character. I daren't cast a stone at anyone, because although I didn't *go* to Viktor years ago, my heart went with him, and I never cared enough about the life I should have been living in London.'

'But you had every excuse! With me away at school and college, and Father on one of his countless retreats—'

'None of that excused *me*, and I'm so happy now that it scares me a bit. Darling, if I never gave you any advice worth having before, remember this – try to do what is *right*, whether it's what you want to do or not. I failed you in so many ways without meaning to.'

Rowena smiled and clasped her mother's hand. 'I'm quite sure you didn't, but maybe we're both catching up now. Which brings me to your wedding. I just can't go back home before then. I must have been out of my mind even to think of it.'

'But Keith has to get back! And there's the trip you planned across Europe! Have you said anything to him yet?'

'No,' Rowena said evenly, 'but he's a reasonable man, and he'll understand that I'm not leaving you before the ceremony. He's got me for the rest of my life, and as for our trip, I'll go maybe as far as Zagreb and then come back. Don't – don't you want me to stay?'

'Of *course* I want you to stay! But I hate spoiling your plans and maybe upsetting Keith.'

Rowena gave a light-hearted chuckle. 'Angel, I wouldn't marry a man who could be upset over anything like this! Well, sweet dreams, and we'll drive you over to Viktor in the morning. I'll take Keith for a long walk, and I'll tell him I'm staying on. It will be all right – you'll see.'

But Anne was still looking thoughtful and a little anxious long after Rowena had gone to her own room.

4

When Keith parked the car in the same place as the day before, Simon came to meet them and kissed Anne on the cheek.

'You slept well?' he asked, mischief in his laughing glance. 'Viktor went to bed singing, and he got up singing, and it is too much for everyone else to bear!' He looked a question at the other two as they made no move to follow him and Anne. 'You are not coming also? Not even for coffee?'

Keith turned and pointed to the woods some miles away. 'We're going to explore in that direction. Even if it gets much hotter, there should be plenty shade among the trees.'

'The woods are very pleasant,' Simon agreed, and Rowena was the only one who happened to be looking at him and saw the sudden perturbation in his expression. 'They are further away than they seem, and after you leave the car there will be three miles to walk. By the time you return, you will have walked six miles – more than enough for this time of day. May we expect you for lunch?'

'No, thank you,' Keith said promptly. 'We'd rather not tie ourselves down to any particular time, but we'll see you all now and again.'

His smile and nod were almost ones of dismissal, and he tucked his arm through Rowena's and led her back to the car. Simon hesitated before he turned away, and Rowena was left wondering what he had been going to say.

The woods *were* further away than they had thought, but it was a beautiful day, with sunlight sparkling on the very blue sea and on the shining crags of the mountains away to their right. The walking was easy because the narrow track had once been a decent road, and the tufts of grass and small flowers now growing all over it only smoothed out roughness in the small stones. Keith loved walking, and as they went along with fingers linked, Rowena told him that she would be staying on until after her mother was married. He said nothing to begin with, and she found herself explaining why she couldn't go with him at the end of his holiday, repeating herself, and becoming rather breathless in the end.

'You – you do see that I can't do anything else?' she asked at last.

Keith laughed shortly, and stopped to light a cigarette. 'I see that you probably intended to stay from the beginning. What I can't understand is why you allowed me to make all those plans for us both to travel home together and take several days over it.'

'You're not being fair! I made the arrangements with you, and I fully expected to – to be free to leave with you. It's not my fault that Mother has to get untangled from red tape before she can get married!'

'No, but it's something you might have expected. Even the Americans with all their high-flown talk about freedom won't let just anyone drop in and marry one of their nationals. No more will the British, who demand at least a residence qualification for a time. And even if you *hoped* you'd be free to come back with me, didn't you give up your job to ensure your having plenty of time if you did decide to stay?'

'No, I did not!' Rowena said crossly. 'It just seemed to be a good time to leave, and you know it! You're being plain mean about this, and it's not as if it involved anything vital. We don't have to postpone our own wedding, or – or move house, nor do we have to be together in London for anything special within the next few weeks. All right, I'm sorry I'll be late getting back, but it isn't my fault!'

She swung away from him and walked ahead, angry tears stinging her eyes as she recalled her own words to her mother the previous night – that Keith was a reasonable man and that he would understand why she couldn't possibly go home with him.

'Darling, I'm sorry,' Keith said as he caught up with her and put an arm round her waist. 'I was disappointed, and I took it out on you, and you're quite right to say I was mean! Of course you must wait and see your mother married, and I only wish I could stay too. I – well, I think I've been a bit afraid you would get too attached to this place. You were so fascinated by that house, you admitted you wanted to give them a hand to get the new rooms ready, and you told me yesterday you were very curious about the different kind of life Viktor and Simon had always led. You know, I think I've been jealous!'

Rowena turned to face the laughter and the hint of anxiety in his blue eyes, and she relaxed.

'Jealous?' she echoed, and smiled. 'I never knew you could be! We're both sorry our arrangements aren't going to work out perfectly, but at least we can enjoy ninety per cent of our holiday. Oh look, the track goes right through the woods – I could just do with some shade!'

It was cool and fragrant among the pine trees, and they had been strolling along for some time, deep in discussion of their own future, when Rowena saw bright sunlight at the edge of the woods, and the outlines of buildings.

'How quiet it is,' she said uncertainly. 'I had no idea there was a village out here. It's too early for siesta, and you'd think we could hear . . .'

Her voice tailed off as her mouth suddenly went dry, and she and Keith halted at the edge of a scene of destruction. The good stone walls of the houses were still standing, but the windows were empty, the roofs were gone, and the scorch marks of long-dead fires threw evil shadows on every home. Time had not been kind to these ruins, washing them white again, or covering them gently with weeds. The charred timbers seen through gaping doorways seemed to have just stopped burning, the pock marks of bullets on the church wall looked fresh, and the great splash of russet colour on the floor inside was scarlet in the shaft of a sunbeam.

'Come away,' Keith said urgently. 'I've never – it's the most terrible place I've ever seen – it should have been bulldozed into the ground long ago! Talk about haunted! Rowena – where are you going?'

'These flowers are fresh,' she said in a whisper, as she dropped to her knees in front of a house. She straightened the glass jar, and touched the flowers with trembling fingers. 'People must come here often. Look, there are little vases at nearly every doorway, and candles stuck in bottle tops. I wonder which house was Simon's?'

'*Simon's?* What on earth are you talking about?'

'But I told you, Keith. Don't you remember? He was only nine, and he saw it all from the edge of the wood where he was hiding in a tree. His mother and his three brothers were shot, and then the house was set on fire over them.' She moved slowly across the dusty road and looked right into the church which was now only a small circle of stone walls. 'The Germans herded about a hundred people in here, and then set the place alight.'

She stared down at the splash of faded red just beyond the doorway, hearing the cries and appeals for mercy intermingled with the stutter of gunfire, smelling the smoke and the flame, and feeling the sorrow which would always

55

be in that place. She held tightly to a projecting stone as the scene came alive before her, and then the pictures faded back to the empty silence of the present, and at last into a blessed oblivion.

She opened her eyes and found that she was lying in the shade at the edge of the wood, and as memory returned, she winced and stared up into the green branches of a fir tree. Keith came hurrying back to her, a soaking handkerchief in his hand, and he sighed with relief as he knelt beside her.

'Thank heaven you've come round! There's a stream over there, but I don't think you'd better drink any water from this horrible place. The water runs towards the village, so at least it hasn't passed through that hell-hole. They've no damn business leaving a sight like that for tourists to come on unawares!'

'I doubt that many come this way,' Rowena murmured as she sat up and wiped her face with the cool, wet handkerchief. "And judging by the flowers and the candles, this is the only memorial the locals have to their friends who died here.'

'It's sheer barbarism!' Keith snapped. 'It made you pass out like a light, and I doubt you've done that often in your life!'

'Never,' Rowena agreed, and stood up. 'All right, darling, you needn't hold me up. I didn't faint from weakness. I suddenly got such a vivid picture of what had happened here, that my mind couldn't grasp any more. I've read about violence, and I've seen it in films, but I've never been in contact with it before. I've always believed it was dreadful of people to go and brood over places like Dachau and Buchenwald—'

'And it *is* dreadful of them! It makes them go on nursing memories of death and brutality twenty years after it was all over and done with! People's minds will

56

never turn towards peace while they keep on resenting and remembering every battle from nineteen-fourteen until nineteen-forty-five. *All* the nations who fought were guilty of bloodlust and cruelty, and from what your mother's told us of the partisans of Yugoslavia, they were the wildest of the lot!'

Rowena frowned towards the stark, empty houses, and then turned and walked back along the track. 'Maybe, but this was their own country, and this was the kind of thing the invader did from end to end of it. Wouldn't you have gone a bit wild too?'

'No,' Keith said as he fell into step beside her. 'If the invaders told me that the price of killing one of their men would be the death of a hundred of my people, I would step very quietly indeed. It's all very well being brave for yourself, but when it means the death of all your family and friends, oh no! Nothing is worth having that on your conscience.'

'I couldn't stand that part of it either,' Rowena said with a small sigh, and curled her fingers in his. 'Oh well, I suppose one shouldn't judge what others do in a time of crisis. You have to be in the same position yourself to know how you would react to the same pressures.'

Keith watched her anxiously, but she managed not to show that her knees had a tendency to shake, and her steps to waver. The track was too narrow for the car, or Keith would have left her in the wood and hurried on ahead for it. Rowena gritted her teeth and kept going . . . two miles to go . . . one mile to go . . . and there was Simon coming slowly to meet them.

His look at Rowena was searching, and she gave him a faint smile and wondered what she could say. He had, after all, grown up in that terrible village, but it was too late for sympathy, and neither the time nor the place for censure. But Keith had no such inhibitions.

'That's right,' he said abruptly. 'She saw your charnel-house, and she passed out. Not a nice experience for your former allies, so how do you think your former enemies will feel? Your uncle said yesterday that all your advance bookings were from Germans. Are you giving them conducted tours up to that place?'

Simon glanced from his angry eyes to Rowena's strained expression, and he shrugged lightly. 'I am very sorry that you were upset. To most people, the sight brings sorrow rather than anger. As for the Germans, there are no indications in the village that the deed was done by them, and if they see the place, no doubt they will blame the Italians, or the Albanians, or the Hungarians, or the Bulgarians, or the Croation Ustashi. These all invaded our country, and they all had their – their charming ways of annihilating the Serbs. Also, it is impossible for the German mind to believe that Germans could ever have been wrong. Betrayed, perhaps, or badly-led, or victims of circumstance, but never never wrong.'

'That's the most sweeping statement I've ever heard,' Keith said as he opened the car door for Rowena. 'You can't dismiss a whole nation like that!'

'We had a long time to learn about them,' Simon said quietly, and Rowena shivered a little as his eyes darkened with memory. 'I am sorry that you will not stay with us for lunch, but you are always welcome when you wish to come.'

Keith gave him a brief nod and got behind the wheel. 'Thank you. Some other time.'

They drove back towards their hotel, and Rowena gave Keith a reproachful glance. 'You were rather rude – most unlike you!'

'I know, and I'm sorry, but I can't stand uncivilised people. The eye-for-an-eye creed, and the harbouring of grudges, and the national pride all give me the horrors, and that young man has more than his fair share of them. But he's got nothing to do with us, so let's forget him. You, my fair lady, are going to have a light lunch, and then a siesta, and we'll see how you feel by dinner time tonight.'

'What will you do all afternoon?'

'Swim, sunbathe, be lazy. It's much too hot for you to snooze on the beach, even in the shade, and you'll be better off in your room with the shutters closed.'

Rowena agreed with a fervour that surprised herself. She would normally feel that a sleep in the afternoon on holiday was a terrible waste of time, but she felt so drained by her experience of the morning that she could hardly wait until lunch was over to get away by herself. Keith adjusted her windows so that the air was cool and the light shaded, kissed her lightly, and went off to the beach.

Her tiredness, and the wine she had had with lunch, made her drop off to sleep more quickly than she had expected, and when she wakened, she saw her mother sitting in an armchair by the window. She took a few moments to remember the events of the day, and then she looked quickly at her travelling clock.

'Mother! Why are you back so early?'

'It's all right, darling, it's almost dinner-time, and I don't have to spend every waking hour with Viktor!' She came over and sat on the edge of the bed, faint anxiety in her eyes. 'Simon told me about – about this morning. I'm so sorry. I would have warned you if I had known.'

'Simon knew, and he never said a word.'

Anne sighed. 'In the first place, he didn't think you would walk quite that far, and in the second place, he could hardly have guessed that you and Keith were the kind to prefer not to know about things like that. He has never been able to shut his eyes to anything, and I suppose he's not used to meeting people who can do that.'

'You're not being quite fair,' Rowena murmured as she

got up. 'I've never met any horrors in my life that I had to shut my eyes *to*. It has never been more than an academic question with me, and it was so easy to say that people shouldn't dwell on the past. Until this morning. No, it wasn't an attack of ladylike faintness. I can't explain it. I was *there*, and it was all happening, and I *heard* it, and I couldn't take it any more. It – it was as if I were Simon, watching it all from the branches of that tree. I – I hope he was able to shut his eyes that day.'

She shook her head, as if to clear the pictures away, and went over to the wash-basin.

'I see,' Anne said thoughtfully. 'Does Keith know that this was how the village affected you?'

'I told him, but even if he heard me, he wouldn't have believed it. We'll just avoid the subject in future. I see his point of view quite clearly, you know, and it would have been mine too if I hadn't *felt* the past so close to me this morning. Was it what Simon said that sent you after me?'

'Well, yes. I think he was afraid that you were both so upset that you would leave at any minute. He asked me to – to smooth things over if I could, so that you would be willing to stay on for the wedding.'

Rowena slipped a cream silk jersey dress over her head. 'I think you'd better tell him it wasn't that kind of "upset." I don't want him to believe – well, anyway, tell him what you like, as long as we don't have to have any more discussion about it.'

'Of course, dear,' Anne said in a non-committal voice, and when Rowena cast her a sharp look, she was buffing her nails on the palm of her hand.

Keith had seen Anne when she arrived back at the hotel, and now he was waiting for them in the lounge. They stood in the doorway for a moment, watching the animated group he was with before he saw them and hurried over. His friends were six young Germans he had met on the beach that afternoon, and Anne laughed at him when he seemed chary of introducing them.

'I won't bite,' she assured him, 'and anyway, my German is getting rusty, and I could do with some practice.'

They had dinner and spent the rest of the evening together, with Anne at her witty and light-hearted best. Rowena commented on her fluent German with some surprise, and Anne pointed out that she had had no opportunity of using it in the last few years. She suggested that learning Serbo-Croatian would be much more of a challenge, and one of the Germans told her that there was really no need to learn it as so many Yugoslavs spoke German.

'But,' said Anne lightly, 'don't you think it's only polite to learn the language of the country you're going to live in? And no foreign language can give you the flavour of a country's literature or thought, or even of its everyday life.'

They agreed that as she was going to live in Yugoslavia, there was some point in getting to know the language, but with German so widely-spoken, there was no need for visitors to understand anything else. Anne smiled pleasantly, and said no more, and Rowena watched and listened with some amusement as she manipulated the conversation and gave eager attention to all the answers and attitudes brought to the surface.

'Fascinating evening,' she murmured as she went upstairs with Keith and Rowena later. 'Thanks for letting Mum join the kids!'

'Nice bunch,' Keith agreed. 'Isn't it better to judge a nation by the present generation, rather than the last?'

'Oh, indeed, yes,' Anne said. 'That's just what I was doing. And they scare me silly. Such a terrifying assurance of being right, then, now, and for ever. Good night, my dears, and you needn't run me over to Srebro Kara in the

61

morning. Viktor is coming, and he'll bring me back at night too.'

She kissed each of them, and went off to her own room, leaving Keith staring after her with a baffled expression.

Rowena laughed softly. 'Don't say it, darling! She's so enjoying saying the unexpected thing these days, and we simply mustn't rise to her every time. Now, about tomorrow, would you like to go to Cetinje with those others?'

'Well, we do want to see the view from the top of Mount Lovčen, but we can go any day. I mean, we don't have to go with a crowd if you'd rather not.'

'Don't mix me up with Mother in your mind! I liked Willi and Marta and Gunther and all the others, so let's join up with them, shall we? And if we find it works out all right, we can go to Dubrovnik with them too.'

Keith was more than ready to agree. The Germans spoke enough English, and he and Rowena enough German for everyone to get on very well. Willi in particular was funny and rather charming, and they were all well-travelled and intelligent.

The view from the twenty-fifth hairpin bend near the top of Lovčen was breathtaking. Kotor Fiord was about four thousand feet below, small towns and villages strung out like jewels along the edge of the still, blue water.

There were three cars in their own party, and several more ahead and behind. Cameras clicked and whirred, snatches of English conversation wafted on the breeze to meet snatches of German and French and Italian. A touring coach hooted for space, and there was a scattering of sightseers, a slamming of car doors, and the starting of engines.

'I wonder how it would be without all this racket,' Rowena said as Keith drove on. 'I suppose we were just unlucky to get there at the same time as so many other people.'

He glanced at her in surprise. 'Tourism is about the biggest industry this country has – or so I've been told. You're bound to find people all over the place. Honestly, darling, don't you think you're being a little unreasonable to find fault with others for doing what you're doing too?'

'Of course I'm being unreasonable!' She paused for a moment, amazed at her own feelings of resentment. 'A place like this should be met with silence and – and sheer wonder. It's so incredibly beautiful you can't believe it – you want to thank somebody or something for being able to look at it. None of those people were looking! They were consulting all the gadgets on their cameras, peering through view-finders, posing their friends against the sky and the mountains!'

'Angel, different places affect different people! I've been much more staggered in the Dolomites than I was here. Anyway, I'm not at all sorry that I got several good shots of you with *my* camera! There's one of you staring into space – talk about "silent upon a peak in Darien"!'

Rowena chuckled and threw off her blue mood. 'I'll admit to an interest in seeing that one! Sorry, Keith, I'll love my fellow-man better when I've had lunch – maybe my subconscious is afraid there won't be room at the hotel in Cetinje!'

Keith agreed that he was feeling hungry too, and then he had to concentrate on his driving, because although the road was good, it was narrow, and they began to meet more local people walking beside laden donkeys. Rowena gazed out at the harsh, bare rock of Montenegro, at the scattered patches of grass and tough bushes, the lonely stone dwellings, the ravines and the rivers. It was wild and unwelcoming, and she loved it, and her heart went out to the women with the proud faces who walked these mountains with such light feet. In the opinion of the great world, they had so little, not even the soil and the climate which made the

63

difference between poverty and prosperity. Whence then came that nobility of bearing, that serenity, that flash of laughter in green eyes and dark eyes, which said that there was always something worth looking for on the far side of the hill?

'Cetinje,' Keith said as they drove into a valley. 'I must say that for a former capital of Montenegro, it looks a bit dull.'

'Sad,' Rowena said thoughtfully, 'not dull. Look at all these former embassies, all bare flagpoles, and not a diplomat in sight. By this street map, that's the royal palace over there. It must all have been very gay, very colourful, once upon a time. Now King Nicholas is dead, Montenegro isn't a kingdom any more, and the capital is a ghost town full of museums.'

Keith drew up outside the hotel and turned to look at Rowena. 'Where *did* you get all that? You sound like a revivalist preacher on the vanities of the world!'

'I was reading some of the hotel books last night,' she said lightly, and laughed a little. 'I've always been a push-over for mountains, and Montenegro is the mountain kingdom of all the fairy tales I've ever read. The very sound of it has bugles and – and bells, and trumpets in it.'

'Strike a light!' Keith said inelegantly. 'Come and get fed, woman, before Romance robs you of your appetite! This holiday was an excellent idea – I'm finding out all kinds of surprising things about you!'

And I about myself, Rowena thought as she got out of the car. It's like – like having new eyesight. I'm seeing 'all things new' like the man in the Bible, and I don't know if I like it or not. What's done this to me? Why should I wonder what's going on in the mind of a peasant woman who looks at me as if I were a curious creature from another world?

She had no answer to give herself, and when she and

64

Keith joined the other members of the party in the dining-room, she had to make an effort to shake off her intro-spection and to appear as lively and full of talk as every-body else. Nobody seemed to notice that it was an effort, and when they drove on to Budva on the coast, Keith was still laughing over some of Willi's jokes. Rowena was laughing too, but as the road snaked down from the heights, she looked back wistfully at the mountain ranges which were darker than ever against a sky paling from blue to lemon and then to pale green flushed with pink. The days were still short, there was very little dusk, and when they reached the ferry at Lepetane it was full dark, with stars beginning to twinkle over the mountain tops.

The ferry could carry two small cars at the same time, and as Rowena stood beside Keith at the rail, she tucked her arm in his. 'Thanks for a lovely day,' she said grate-fully. 'All that driving must have been tiring for you, but for your passenger it was quite fabulous!'

'Oh, I rather enjoyed it all myself. I love driving, and I could still take in a lot of the scenery. But maybe we should have a day off tomorrow? Just swim and laze around.'

Rowena agreed, knowing that the Germans intended to do the same. She felt a little guilty over not having gone again to Srebro Kara, but it was the same old story of not being able to please everyone all the time. Perhaps Keith wouldn't mind if she went there with her mother in the morning. He could call for her with the car in time for lunch, he'd have had company on the beach all morning, and he wouldn't have had to waste time with Viktor and Simon with whom he had so little in common.

As it happened, Keith understood very well how she felt, and his only anxiety was that she shouldn't mind too much that he wasn't going too.

'They're just not my kind of people,' he explained

65

ruefully, 'and I don't want to upset your mother by looking bored with them, or by getting into an argument!'

'Which would be more than likely,' Rowena agreed. 'It's much more sensible of us to arrange it this way, and at least I know I'm not leaving you on your own. See you about one o'clock.'

Viktor was pleased to have her for the morning, and as she sat in the back of the jeep, she watched her mother with amusement. Anne kept glancing at Viktor as if she still couldn't quite believe it was all true, and judging by the upward tilt at the corner of Viktor's mouth, he was well aware of it.

What fun they're going to have together, Rowena thought. So much love, so much gratitude that they had found each other again. How they would cherish what was between them for the rest of their days.

Simon was putting the final polish on the new reception desk when they arrived, and Rowena was surprised at the amount that had been done in just two days. The wall behind the desk now had a key-board with twenty pigeon-holes all tagged with the room numbers, and there was a notice-board full of information about local events, coach and boat tours, beauty-spots, and where to buy which kind of souvenir. Each notice was printed in German, English, French and Italian, and Rowena thought that her own hotel could take a lesson there.

Anne took Rowena all over the place, something for which there didn't seem to have been time before. On the top floor of the house, she opened the door of a corner bedroom and stood aside.

'This has always been Viktor's room,' she said, 'and we've decided to keep it for ourselves. In fact, this floor will only be for "family," which includes Simon and Natalya, of course, but there's also a spare room for family friends. Like you, maybe!'

'Which one?' Rowena asked, and when Anne pointed, she went into the room next door and crossed to the window. It overlooked the front, and she gazed out at the glittering blue of the sea, and at the dark eternal mountains far away against the sky. She turned to inspect the room itself, approving of the white walls and white paint and the brilliant embroidered covers on the bed and the chair. There was one other splash of colour, an ikon of delicately-painted green and pink and grey on the wall, a figure with great, calm eyes, and a finely modelled mouth.

'The Angel of Mileševo,' Anne said. 'Viktor told me she's on a thirteenth-century fresco in the Monastery of Mileševo – I think it's called "The Angel at Christ's Grave." He keeps her in here because he believes that strangers would like her.'

'How dear of him,' Rowena said, looking long at the brooding, serene face. 'He's more generous than I am. I'd keep her for myself. I – I'd like to be the "family friend" to stay in this room, but I can't see it happening.'

'Oh, but you must come here after Keith leaves! Don't try to extend your booking at the hotel – come straight here and stay until after the wedding, or until you want to go home.'

'Don't tempt me to make my life one long holiday,' Rowena said with a smile. 'I'll have no excuse at all to stay on after you're married, and anyway, I've got my own wedding to think about. Will there be any chance of your being there?'

Anne sighed unhappily. 'Darling, you've no idea how much thought I've been giving to that. I couldn't bear *not* to be there, but, and I know this sounds quite mad, I'm scared to move anywhere without Viktor. If he could come too, if only I didn't ever have to lose sight of him again . . .'

'Darling, I do understand,' Rowena said, and gave Anne a quick hug as they went towards the stairs. 'I honestly think I'd rather you stayed here, where I know everything's turned out so beautifully for you. If I can arrange the date so that it's not within the hotel season, maybe Viktor would like to see London again. But we can think about all that later.'

Natalya had coffee waiting in the small sitting-room, but she soon returned to the kitchen, and Viktor and Anne went off to inspect a bale of new curtain material which had just arrived. Simon poured more coffee, and smiled across at Rowena.

'How did you like your day out yesterday?' he asked. 'You were lucky it was clear – sometimes the clouds come right down over the mountains, and it is very disappointing for people who have only the one chance of seeing that view.'

'I wish I could have seen it all by myself,' Rowena said, remembering her frustration of the previous day. 'I know it's quite unreasonable, and selfish, and plain uncharitable, but I could cheerfully have swept everyone out of my sight! It was such a tower of Babel, and so many of these people were a blot on the landscape. Sure, it was warm, but men in vests, and women in strapless suntops were – were sheer sacrilege up there! It was only bad taste anyway, because it couldn't have been comfort that made them add baggy trousers and tight-waisted skirts. A man in shorts and nothing else can look quite decent, but in his *undervest* – revolting!'

She was laughing too, as she saw the dancing amusement in his expression, and he told her that she could expect the same thing in Dubrovnik or any other place that was packed with tourists. He was used to it now, but there had been a time when he had goggled at creased plastic macs, sun-raw women bulging out of brief dresses, and shorts which were unkind to the legs of both sexes.

'If they'd only taken a good look at some of the local

women yesterday,' Rowena said dreamily. 'I suppose their dark dresses were what you might call shapeless, but they walked so beautifully, and they *belonged* there as outsiders never could.'

'Would it have been more pleasant if you had been surrounded by such people, rather than by your outsiders?'

His question was asked in a careful, casual voice, but Rowena never noticed that as she sat forward with eager interest.

'Oh, *yes*. And I'd have listened to them as well as looked around me, only I'd have been sorry not to have known their language, and I'd have made up my mind to learn it – in fact, I'm going to learn it anyway. I'd have wanted to know all about them, and about their lives, and I'd hope they might like me too . . .' Her voice tailed off, and she stared at Simon with some of her eagerness fading away. 'Why did you ask me that?'

He reached across the table and covered her hand with his. 'Because it sounded to me as if you were falling in love with this place and with this people. I thought of myself at your Tower of London perhaps, and I would be impatient with the Americans and the Dutch and the Germans around me only because they were not English, because they were aliens in a place that I loved. I would forget that *I* was an alien also, remembering only that I wished to keep England and the English for myself.'

'Oh, no!' Rowena gasped with dismay, and she jumped to her feet. 'I'm only here for a little while, and I could never get involved like – like you said. It's just that this is my kind of scenery, and that I'm interested in all kinds of people.'

But not in the alien people of yesterday, she told herself with a sinking heart. Not as she was interested in the waiters at her own hotel, in the chambermaid who chattered to her in a mixture of German and Italian and

English, in everyone who passed her on the roads. It had all 'grown' on her so suddenly, this absorption in a people who had been strangers to her a week before.

'And the language?' Simon asked gently. 'Serbo-Croatian is not the easiest one to learn, and the labour is worth it only if one is to spend a lot of time here, or unless one does it for love.'

'I forgot about the time I'd be here. I just wanted to know the language.' She took a few steps about the room, and then exclaimed: 'One *can't* fall in love with a whole nation!'

'Why not?' Anne asked gaily, as she and Viktor returned.

Rowena's gaze was unseeing, and she thought of the years ahead when the country would be lost to her as if she had never known it. Keith wouldn't come back, and if she came alone it would only be for brief glimpses, like a lover who had delighted in the dawn of an affair, and then grown old without ever knowing fulfilment.

5

LATER that day, Rowena came out of the water to find some shade on the sandy beach below her hotel. Keith was swimming out in the bay, Marta was lying in full sunlight while Gunther oiled her tanned shoulders, and everyone else was far enough away to leave an oasis of quiet where Rowena lay with her head on her crossed arms, under a beach umbrella.

When Keith had called for her at Srebro Kara that morning, they had all met him in the garden and passed a few moments in discussing pleasant trivialities. No one had mentioned her stunned acceptance of the fact that she would be leaving much of her heart behind her when she finally left Yugoslavia.

'I was what you might call conditioned, because of Viktor,' Anne had said thoughtfully, 'and so I was ready to love his country and his people, as I do. But I believe it would be just as easy to feel the same, coming on the place "cold," and without having any previous convictions about it.'

Viktor laughed. 'Like myself and the Gurkhas! I did some of my training with them in England, and I loved every little man in that battalion. They were loyal, tough, cheerful, and some of them were devils – not at all perfect, no! – but love does not look for perfection. It just arrives, and there is nothing that one can do about it.'

'I'm doomed anyway,' Rowena said lightly. 'It seems to run in my family! Look at Uncle Oliver who has thought of the Serbs as his band of brothers ever since Salonika in the First War. He even managed to get back here in the middle of the last war, and had himself a whale of a time fighting in the mountains!'

So it had all passed off lightly on the surface, and now she had to take stock. She was being romantic and soft, neither of which she had ever been in her life. Her future was all mapped out, and it was a good and satisfying one with the man she loved. Now that she came to think of it, an awful lot of people had had romantic dreams about faraway places. There was Xanadu, and Babylon, and Ispahan, and the Hesperides, and Avalon, and there were Flecker's marvellous lines about the Golden Journey to Samarkand.

Rowena lifted her head and looked towards the east where Montenegro's mountains were dark blue near the frontier. The words of the Golden Journey echoed in her mind.

'We are the Pilgrims, Master, we shall go
Always a little further; it may be
Beyond that last blue mountain barred with snow . . .'

Beyond it, and into Serbia and Macedonia, into regions that could only be names now, like the beckoning sound of distant bells. Sure, but the poets had gone on with their daily lives just the same, and Bokhara and Tyre and rose-red Petra were just dreams for an idle moment.

Rowena laughed softly at her own deep thoughts. She had never been a dreamer, and it had caught her unawares, that was all.

She tried to remember that on the following day, when she and Keith and the six young Germans went to Dubrovnik. There were only two cars in the party this time, and as Willi and Marta travelled with them, Rowena didn't talk as much as she might have done. Willi was a great conversationalist, and as he kept going for most of

72

the thirty miles, Rowena's contented quietness went unnoticed. She wasn't even aware of it herself, so absorbed was she in the farms of the Konavle valley, and in the people who lived there. She responded gaily to waves from children outside a school, and she and Marta both gasped over the embroidered dresses of some women being photographed by tourists from a coach.

Dubrovnik was a much-pictured town, and familiar to all of them, but the first sight of it was enough to silence even Willi. The sea was so very blue where it surrounded the golden-white walls on three sides, the red-tiled roofs glowed russet in the brilliant light, and bell-towers vied with church domes for a place against the sky.

'There isn't much anyone can do to spoil a place like that,' Rowena said at last. 'They can only build well outside the walls, and leave that gem for a few more hundred years.'

There was no wheeled traffic permitted in the old town, and after they had parked the cars, the eight young people went over the drawbridge and through the gate at the head of the long main street, the Placa. It was difficult to gain much impression of the town because it was so crowded with holiday-makers. There were also many groups of twenty or more, led by official guides who lectured about the museums, the churches, the monasteries, the fountains. The shops on each side of the Placa were crammed to the doors, and when the party reached the old harbour, several launches came in from a cruise liner with a drove of passengers determined to 'do' Dubrovnik in about an hour.

Simon had advised them to lunch early and then to make their way round the places they wanted to see. By two o'clock, the town seemed almost empty, the holiday crowds had gone to their hotels, the shops were shut, and the passengers had returned to their liner.

'This is better,' Keith said after he and Rowena had

detached themselves from the others, and gone into the Franciscan cloisters. 'I was beginning to see what you meant by being up to the neck in tourists!'

They sat on a warm stone bench amid flowers and trees, and looked at the old, carved walls of the monastery.

'As you also pointed out,' Rowena said, 'we're tourists ourselves! There's no answer to this overcrowding of the world's lovely places today. Everyone's entitled to see them, and if everyone gets there at the same time – well, that's just too bad!'

It was what a reasonable woman could be expected to say, but it didn't mean that that was what she felt. She didn't want to share Dubrovnik with anyone except the people who lived there, and they certainly wouldn't thank her for wishing the place empty of tourists. They would have very lean purses indeed, were it not for the crowds of strangers who poured into the country every year from all over the world.

'Why don't you care for this country?' Rowena asked suddenly. 'I remember one of our protest demonstrations outside the American Embassy – you were quite convinced of the truth of your slogan, which was "Better to be Red than Dead." Well, the Reds won this country for themselves during the war, and they've kept it, and they don't try to spread their beliefs outside their own borders.'

'They're not out-and-out Reds,' Keith said with faint scorn. 'I'd respect them more if they were. They're not even an outright dictatorship, nor are they a democracy. You can't place them anywhere.'

'I find that very inconsistent. This is a republic, and it works. Anyway, why do you find Austria, for example, so much more to your taste?'

They strolled out again to the Placa, and walked in the shade towards the harbour at the far end. Keith thought about the question, and then he shrugged.

74

'It's this business of civilisation again. I would call Austria a civilised country, but Yugoslavia still has too far to go in that direction to suit me. Except for commercialism. This town may have been worth studying fifty years ago, but now it's just a shop-window, a tripper's paradise where almost everything can be bought apart from the stone the place is built of.'

'But people have to live, and what else have they got? You've seen the soil around here – it can't support much in the way of food or livestock, and they can't build factories on this strip of coast. Anyway, it was the Austrians who ruled this part of the country fifty years ago, and you can't say that the Hapsburgs as colonisers were anything to be proud of! The Italians and the Hungarians and the Turks ruled the rest of the country, so don't you think they were more to blame than the Slavs for any lack of civilisation?'

Keith laughed with genuine amusement. 'Oh, darling, you've been digging in that hotel bookcase again! It's common sense to believe that those other nations were responsible for any modernity or good taste this country happens to have.'

Rowena turned at the Clock Tower, and looked from the Gothic arches of the Rector's Palace to the Renaissance windows of the Sponza Palace, then back along the Placa lined with tall, gracious houses, to the Franciscan monastery.

'Twelfth century onwards,' she said softly, 'and the Austrians didn't grab the Illyrian Provinces until eighteen-fifteen. So who worked all this beauty with native architects and native labour? The Slavs. And who started schools and orphanages and hospitals, and abolished the slave trade in the fifteenth century? The native people of this country. It makes you think – we British didn't even dream of abolishing the slave trade until the nineteenth century. How's that for civilisation?'

75

Keith opened his mouth to speak, shut it again, and looked across at the ancient Pillar of Orlando.

'You are an irritating woman,' he said after a moment, and Rowena's smile faded as his brilliant blue eyes narrowed. 'All right, you've been lapping up guide-books, and you know it all. But get this into your head – I don't want to argue about this country. I'm quite happy to know nothing about it, because it doesn't interest me in the slightest. I'm enjoying the climate, the hotel is comfortable, and the food is good, but that's as far as my preferences go. On that basis, do you think we can get through our remaining days without more cultural lectures?'

Rowena had never seen him so annoyed, and in honesty she had to admit that it was her own fault. In a childish way, she had enjoyed scoring off him over the Austrians, but she should have remembered the burned-out village, and the dislike Keith had taken to Simon and to what he called Yugoslav national pride.

'I'm sorry,' she said in a small voice. 'I find it all very interesting, and I – I just wanted to talk about it. I should have thought of my school trip to Madrid! I just couldn't like the place, or get excited about any of the excursions, and the teacher in charge of us was so cross with me because I couldn't hide my boredom. At least you've been very good at hiding yours!'

He sighed and his mouth relaxed in a smile. 'I'm not bored. I'm a sun-worshipper, and I'm getting plenty of that here. I'm sorry I got mad at you, but it was just – well, like the case of you and Madrid!'

The small storm was over, and they strolled through to sit on the harbour wall until the gates leading up to the ramparts opened again after the siesta. As Keith said, with a teasing glance, they might as well go the whole hog and see everything that tourists were supposed to see. Rowena replied with equal lightness, and for a time they wrangled amicably about the merits of Brighton or Edinburgh for their short honeymoon later in the year.

But something had gone from the bright day, and even when they joined up with Willi and the others, Rowena found herself being careful of what she said. She wanted to exclaim with delight as she looked down from the ramparts into the green cloister of the Dominicans, to gaze raptly at old, crooked, pink rooftops, and to call everyone to see a courtyard ablaze with flowers and shrubs in every kind of container. At one good vantage point, all the cameras were much in evidence, and while she waited, Rowena turned and looked out across the sea beyond the Fort of St. John.

She was acting a part, she who had always been so sure of herself, and who had so despised women who let their hearts rule their heads. She was changing, and it frightened her, because she hadn't wanted to change, and she didn't know what to do about the new emotions which were assailing her. They had nothing to do with the life to which she would be returning, and somehow she would have to come to terms with the present and the future. And it might pass as suddenly as it had come, this 'love affair with a nation,' which had dismayed her and which Simon had found so easy to understand.

For the remainder of Keith's holiday, they stayed put, apart from picnics to other good bathing beaches. They sailed a lot, and apart from two stormy days, the weather was warm and sunny. Rowena went to Srebro Kara a couple of times, but it wasn't until the day before he left that Keith went with her. They had decided against travelling together for part of the way. Keith could get a direct flight from Cilipi airport to London, and Victor had offered to drive him there and then to take Rowena back to Srebro Kara. Anne's wedding was to be about a week after that, and although Rowena hadn't set a date for her return to London, it was somehow taken for granted that she would arrive about ten days after Keith. She was counting desperately on those ten days to bring her life back to a semblance of normality.

'Nice of Viktor to take me to the airport,' Keith said as he and Rowena drove to Srebro Kara. 'I'll have to turn this car in tonight. Are you sure you wouldn't rather extend your booking where you are? You're bound to get involved in all the preparations for the opening of Srebro Kara if you're staying there.'

'I won't mind that,' Rowena said hastily, 'and anyway, it will give me a chance to see more of Mother. They won't have the time to go away for a honeymoon, so I'll be able to see her in her own home, and be sure that she's settled down all right.'

Keith grinned. 'Just how much proof do you need? She's been settled since the first five minutes! There she is now – hanging her own curtains in her own house!'

Anne waved to them from the first-floor guest rooms, and she met them in the hall when they went inside.

'The drawing-room's finished,' she said excitedly, 'and you must come and see it. We'll have coffee in there – we won't have many more chances once our guests start arriving. You've no *idea* the amount of work there is in running a hotel.'

'No,' Keith said with mock gravity, 'and we're quite happy to leave it to you to find out!'

Anne's giggle was girlish and unaffected, and she didn't look a day over twenty-five as she went out to see about coffee. The big room on the left of the hall was decorated in white as was most of the house, but colour had been supplied by the aquamarine curtains, by the glowing Pirot rugs on the marble floor, and by the comfortable chairs covered in tangerine, and dark coffee, and green.

Natalya joined them after Simon and Viktor had come

in, and they were all sitting talking when Rowena looked out of the window and saw the woman on the donkey. They had stopped outside the front wall, and after the woman had taken stock of the house, she led the donkey to the gate and stood there fondling his ears.

'What a love of a donkey,' Rowena murmured, and Viktor came over to see what she was looking at. 'And what a very beautiful woman. She must be at least sixty, but – so lovely.'

'Yes,' he said with a smile, 'she is, as you say, very lovely. That is my cousin Marija from Izvor. She has come a long way – I wonder why?'

He hurried out to meet her, and Simon took his place at the window.

'She has come to see if there is work for her here,' Simon said, as Viktor kissed his cousin and led the donkey round to the side of the house. 'The new hotel is news in our family circles! Marija is a widow, and she has a pension, but life has not been easy for her. Her husband died in the mountains with the partisans, and her two sons in the Battle for Belgrade.'

Cousin Marija came in with Viktor, and when he explained who Anne was, her thin features seemed to glow with pleasure. Keith bowed courteously over her hand, and Rowena smiled back into eyes that were green and lively and eternally young.

'Can Viktor fit her in?' she asked Simon in an anxious whisper.

'I am sure he will do it somehow. As a chambermaid, perhaps, or as a relief cook to help Natalya.'

'Who are you going to have as receptionist?' Rowena asked urgently.

'Oh – I suppose we shall all do that when it is required. We have no one who can be spared to be at the desk all the time.'

'But how marvellous she would look there. She would give cachet to any establishment, in black with lace collar and cuffs, and that white hair piled on top of her head. What's her name? Talevski? Madame Talevski. How many languages can she speak?'

'Darling,' Keith warned, 'I thought you weren't going to interfere? Viktor knows what he wants to do with his staff.'

'Yes, of course,' Rowena murmured, but Simon was thoughtful, and she knew that he liked her suggestion, and that he would pass it on.

He went over to talk to Natalya, and Rowena watched as the other girl gave him all her attention. How lovely she was, with those dark, deep-set eyes and smooth olive skin, and how brightly affectionate was her glance as she laughed and shook her head at something Simon had said.

'Handsome lot,' Keith murmured, 'in a dark and brooding sort of way! But what makes you think the old cousin is so special? She looks like any aged peasant who's just come in from the fields, and she's not nearly as pretty as your mother, for example.'

'Oh, bone structure, I suppose,' Rowena said vaguely. 'My father had the same kind of looks.'

This was another occasion when it seemed wiser to say little. Marija's upright carriage had sagged as she relaxed in a chair and drank coffee. Her black skirt was dusty round the hem, her stockings were wrinkled, and her woven leather slippers were almost worn out. She was very tired, afraid that her journey might have been in vain, and her work-roughened hands shook slightly round her coffee cup. But to Rowena, she was beauty and dignity and indomitable spirit, and a moment later they exchanged faint, inquisitive smiles.

When they left, Keith went out to the hall with Anne, and Rowena looked back into the room at Marija.

'She will still be here when you come tomorrow,'

Viktor said with a soft laugh. 'Simon told me of your idea, and it is a very good one as far as it goes. Marija can read and write, but she cannot do so in German or Italian although she can understand those languages, and speak them also. She has no English at all, and she would have to learn about passports and registers, and be able to answer the kind of questions which our guests are sure to ask.'

'Perhaps she'd be happier doing bedrooms,' Rowena admitted regretfully. 'I was just thinking of appearances, because the receptionist at our hotel is a grouchy old man. He's competent, but not beautiful, if you see what I mean!'

'Yes, I see,' Viktor said thoughtfully. 'The welcome is important. Perhaps between them, Anne and Marija could manage it. But there is plenty of time to discuss it after tomorrow. I am so glad that you are coming to stay with us.'

She looked up into his kind eyes, and was smitten with envy of her mother. This man would have time and affection to spare for a new daughter of twenty-one, but the relationship wasn't ever going to get the chance to develop. It seemed such a waste, and she gave a wry, inward smile as she recalled with what half-amused relief she had handed her mother over to this atmosphere of abundant affection which she was quite sure she couldn't bear to live with herself.

The following morning, Viktor drove them in the jeep to Cilipi airport. It had rained during the night, and the dust of the roads was laid, and Keith, who had never been in a jeep before, was entranced by its performance and comfort. He had never taken such a vehicle seriously, but it was practically tailor-made for rough country such as one was apt to find in Yugoslavia.

Viktor remained in the car-park while Rowena went to the departure gate with Keith, and after flight formalities they had only a few minutes together. In a light-weight grey suit, he was more the familiar Keith of London, except that he was very sun-bronzed, and that she felt a little at a loss with him.

'I *am* sorry you're having to go back alone,' she said. 'But I can't go away and let Mother get married without me.'

His eyes were clear and his smile was fond as he touched her cheek. 'Of course you can't, my sweet, and it won't be for long anyway. I've a full schedule at the office, so that will help to make the next ten days pass quickly for me. Don't – don't get too involved with your new family, will you? I know you've taken a bit of a header for them, but even if you hadn't any plans of your own, you don't belong here.'

'Oh, no, of course I don't. It's just – I had so many doubts about Mother, and now I'm so pleased for her. All apprehensions laid to rest, as you might say! Oh, that's your flight being called.'

They held each other closely as they kissed, and Rowena took a half-step forward when Keith left her. But everything had been said in that last embrace, and she stayed where she was, her expression thoughtful and faraway, until the plane was out of sight. If Mother's wedding had been over in time, she would have been leaving today with Keith . . . she would have already said a long farewell to this country . . . there would have been no returning to Viktor who waited outside . . .

She was wearing a yellow dress that morning, her smooth brown hair was touched with gold in the sunlight, and her grey eyes held a strange peace. She came to a narrow concrete border before she reached the jeep, and she stepped up on it, balancing carefully as she walked, and then skipping off at the end of it. She looked up when she heard Viktor laughing, and he came forward and grasped her hands.

'You look like a child of fifteen who has run away from school! Where is the serious young woman who arrived here almost two weeks ago?'

'She – she's got a little lost,' Rowena said uncertainly. 'Was she really so serious?'

Viktor kept one of her hands in his and led her to the jeep. 'I thought so then. An earnest young woman, who knew very many things, but *not* by experience. One who believed in a planned, a tidy life without loose ends, one who deplored "sentiment," and who made no allowances for the human heart which will open like a flower when one least expects it. Am I hurting your feelings?'

'No,' she answered gravely, her expression as sober as his. 'You're putting into words something that I haven't been able to work out. I was quite happy to stay as I was, I wouldn't have chosen such – such a flowering among strange people in a strange place. But it was there before I was aware of it, and now I've got to make it fit in with the life ahead of me. Don't mistake me – I'm looking forward to my marriage, to having my own home and family, but what do you do about the piece of human heart you've had to leave a thousand miles away?'

They were sitting in the jeep now, and Viktor leaned on the steering wheel, and ran a hand through his thick white hair. 'You do without it,' he said after a moment. 'In my own case, all I can say is that you do not die of it. That was different, of course, because I left so much of me with one particular person. Anne was the focus of all the longing and yes, I will say it, the pain, and there were times when I felt it could not be borne. It will not be so hard for you because you will be with the person you love, and that is more than enough compensation for anyone.'

He turned and smiled at her. 'We are being very sober! I hope we have not lost the child who ran away from school?'

83

'No,' Rowena said, and her eyes were peaceful again. 'I'm just sort of giving thanks for my extra days here. They are a bonus from the gods, and I'll accept them and enjoy them, and I won't pine for them afterwards.'

Viktor dropped a light kiss on her fingers, and then drove on, and Rowena knew that he doubted her capacity to keep nostalgia at bay. He was aware of Keith's attitude to the people and to the country, and of the fact that Keith's wife would come very seldom, if at all, to Yugoslavia. She had faced up to that already, and she could cope with it. She was sure of that. A fleeting memory of Dryden's lines came to her. 'The joys I *have* possessed are mine . . . not heaven itself upon the past has power; . . . but what has been, has been, and I have had my hour.'

They pulled up at the hotel where Anne was waiting with the luggage, and then went on to Srebro Kara, all three of them ridiculously light-hearted and apt to burst into song. Simon surveyed them with tolerant eyes as he carried Rowena's two suitcases upstairs, and he smiled as she went straight over to the ikon of the Angel of Mileševo.

'Anne told me you liked her,' he said. 'I have one in my room also, but the colours are different. I wonder why we all say "her"? Angels are not supposed to be either male or female!'

'Ah, but no mere man could be so beautiful!'

'The expression of the eyes,' Simon said thoughtfully. 'That is how you look when you see something which pleases you very much – as on the day you went to meet our donkeys, and they all came crowding round you! You go quiet, and serene, just like this Angel. That must be why I have felt all along that I have seen you before.'

'A charming idea,' Rowena murmured, as she stepped back. Simon was still studying the ikon and didn't seem to hear her, and she watched him with frank interest. She too had had a feeling that she must have seen something very like him before. The wide-set dark eyes under winged brows, the prominent cheekbones in the thin, brown face, and those little lines around the mouth – they all added up to something remembered and liked.

'I beg your pardon,' he said, suddenly realising where he was. 'I was in a dream! Rowena, I have been thinking about your disappointment when it was so crowded up on Mount Lovčen. Before you return to England, would you like to see the sun rise from up there? You can be sure that there will be no coaches and cars at that hour!'

'Oh, Simon, could we? What a wonderful idea!'

'I thought perhaps we might go on the night of the wedding? The hotel opens a few days after that, we shall be so busy, and you will be going home. But on that night, we will be late anyway, and we might as well stay up altogether. The ferry will not be running, so we shall have to go all the way round the fiord, which means over thirty miles before we even reach the serpentine road. We would have to leave here before three in the morning.'

'I could even face getting up at that hour,' Rowena said blithely. 'It *is* kind of you to think of this, Simon. But you'll lose a night's sleep – you'll be so tired.'

He laughed softly. 'Somehow I think that we shall all be on holiday the next day! Anyway, it is time that I saw a sunrise over Kotor again. So many times I have thought that I would go, but somehow I never went. I would tell myself that the skies would be heavy, and that I could have seen little!'

'Oh! Then let's pray hard for a beautiful day for the bride and groom, and a beautiful sunrise for us!'

Impulsively, they shook hands on that, and Natalya gave them a curious look as they stood smiling in the doorway. She had just come upstairs, and when Simon told her they were wishing sunshine for the wedding, she threw her hands out and raised her eyebrows.

'Have you *seen* the bridegroom?' she asked. 'He is dancing what he is pleased to call a polka, and he has to uphold the bride who can do nothing but laugh! It will be a miracle if we are able to do any work at all during the week!'

But the work went on, particularly in the evenings when the masons and the carpenters and the painters came to lend a hand.

'You do not find this also a tower of Babel?' Simon asked Rowena one night. She was hanging curtains in the annexe, the din of hammering, voices, and sawing was earsplitting, and to bring her coffee Simon had to step over two prone bodies engaged in smoothing off a floorboard. He was laughing at her as she sat on top of the steps, and she beamed back.

'Oh, but this is *different*! We're all together – we belong and this is going to be *the* most beautiful hotel on the coast! Bless you, European coffee – I don't mind Turkish once in a while, but I don't think I'll ever enjoy it.'

'And slivovica?' he asked wickedly.

'Ah, well, yes, I didn't realise it was quite so potent, did I? Now that *is* an acquired taste. I didn't care for its dryness at first, but it grows on one, and that's why I was weaving slightly when I went to bed last night. I seem to have amused you all mightily.'

'You were so funny,' he said reminiscently. 'You were so shocked at yourself, and really two small glasses cannot do anyone harm. Marija was very cross with us because we teased you. She treats you like her own lost lamb!'

'That's partly because I dressed her hair on top of her head like that. Did you *ever* see such a duchess? But she was more thrilled with my shampoo than with anything – she'd never smelt or used anything like it in her life. I wish I'd brought more of that kind of thing with me, just so that I could leave it with people like Marija.'

86

'You miss such products here?'

'Yes, I do,' she said honestly, 'but that's because I'm used to them. I'm not mad about your soaps and other toilet goods, and imported things are so expensive, but I still think you're all doing fine. In a few more years you'll have all the frivolities you want, and – and maybe it will change you. You might get like us – a bit selfish, and scrambling for the good things of life, and forgetting what you are.'

'And what are we?' He moved closer as an outburst of hammering came from the passage.

She looked down into his eyes from her perch on the steps. 'Oh, very independent, honest with yourselves and with other people, loving in a way that we English could never show outwardly, and – and with the kind of courage that legends are made of.'

'I am glad that we seem like that to you,' he said in a quiet voice. 'I would like to believe it was true.'

Rowena dragged her gaze away and saw her mother at the foot of the steps. Anne glanced from one to the other of them, and then took Rowena's empty cup from her.

'I must get to bed before I fall flat on my face,' she said lightly. 'Rowena, you won't mind if we aren't here tomorrow morning? You could go for a swim, or maybe just have a lie-in. The three of us are going over to the village. She – Viktor was very fond of his sister, and – and she was Simon's mother – and there were the three little boys too. Tomorrow is the day before we get married, and we'd like to take some flowers, and – and there isn't any-where else to put them.'

She put the cup on a chair, Simon looked out of the window, and Rowena thought about the burned houses and the stark shell of the church.

'Can't I come too?' she asked, and they both looked at her with some apprehension. 'If I think I'm going to –

to *hear* anything, I'll stay in the wood. But I'd like to come.'

'I will stay with you,' Simon promised, 'in the village or in the wood. It will be all right.'

Viktor was able to take the jeep as far as the edge of the woods, and the four of them walked the rest of the way among sunbeams slanting through the branches. Rowena took a deep breath as they came in sight of the houses, and her fingers tightened on the two red roses she had picked earlier. Now she knew the house where Simon had been born, and where he had lived for nine years, and she knelt beside him and placed her roses with his. There were no dreadful pictures in her mind this morning, and when Viktor and Anne went to the church, she looked over to the wood.

'It was that big pine,' Simon said, understanding what she was looking for. He took her arm and they walked towards it. 'I have a great affection for this tree which saved my life. And yet . . .' He turned to look at what he had escaped from, and he sighed. 'If I had had more courage, who knows what might have happened?'

'No!' Rowena exclaimed, and saw the boy of nine who had had to be unclasped from the tree when help arrived too late. 'You would only have died too! Oh, no!'

He looked quickly at her, and then held her closely against him, his hand strong and gentle at the back of her head. She shivered in his arms until his soothing voice made her remember that he was there with her. He hadn't died. He had escaped the wholesale murder, and he was alive, most wonderfully alive.

She had stopped shaking, but her hold on him was firm and sure. Her head was pressed against his shoulder, and all she could think of was that the horrors were long past, and that Simon had survived. It was like being present at a miracle. It was like suddenly coming alive herself.

6

It was getting late, but the vinery and reception rooms of
Srebro Kara were still full of people. Anne and Viktor had
been married that afternoon, and now they were just
waiting for a chance to slip away quietly to the deserted
top floor. Natalya was going home for the night with her
mother and sisters, Rowena and Simon would be on the
way to the top of Mount Lovčen, and Marija would be
the only other person staying in the house.

Anne had worn gentian blue, the colour of her eyes,
looking lovelier than Rowena had ever seen her, and now
she was sitting with her hand in Viktor's, listening to a
Montenegrin song which wished them long life and
happiness. Rowena was sitting at a table with Natalya,
and when she sighed a little, the other girl glanced at
her.

'You are tired, Rowena? Or perhaps it is that we both
envy those who were married today! I tell myself that
they have had to wait a long time for their great day, that
they have earned their joy in each other, but to me it is
terrible to have to wait at all.'

They both looked over to the group where Simon was
standing, and he seemed almost a stranger in his dark suit
and polished shoes.

'I wondered —' Rowena began uncertainly. 'I mean,
no one has said anything about you and Simon. Why do
you have to wait?'

'Oh, but we could not get married when I have just come

to be Viktor's housekeeper and cook! He has been so wonderful to my family – we owe him more than I can ever explain to you, and now perhaps we can return a little of his goodness if I do well for him here. It would be unthinkable if I were to marry now and start having babies, and therefore could not do my work! Simon loves children. Do you, Rowena?'

'I – yes, I do. Well, not children in a heap, so to speak, but my husband's and my own, yes. But now that my mother is here too, surely she could cope if – if you did start having a family. She would still have quite a while to learn anything she didn't know from you.'

Natalya's smile was indulgent. 'Oh, but you know how Viktor feels about that. He says that Anne has not come here to be a cook or to take any kind of job in a hotel, that she is his wife alone, and that she must do no more than if she had come to live in a private house. It is understandable. Oh, he will come round later, and Anne will be on our side also, but meanwhile I remind myself that I am but twenty-six, and that Simon is but thirty-one!'

She put her hand on Rowena's and looked at her with faint anxiety. 'You will not mention any of what I have been saying? I could not bear that Viktor should think he was holding us back, that he should feel he was standing in the way of our happiness. Simon loves him as a father, and Simon also would be hurt if he thought that I became too impatient like this sometimes!'

'No, of course I won't say anything,' Rowena told her. 'I know exactly what you mean about people being hurt when it's the last thing one intended. I – I hope you won't have to wait too long, though. You and I might even be getting married about the same time!'

'That is later in the year, is it not? Ah well, we shall have to see what happens. Your Keith will not be willing to wait beyond the appointed time – one could see that he found you the only woman in the world for him! Ah, my family are ready to leave, so I shall see you sometime tomorrow night. It is my first free day for weeks, and it seemed a good occasion on which to be away!'

She stopped to speak to Simon as she crossed the vinery, and Rowena watched them when they went into the house. Maybe the family would have to wait for some time yet. Rowena was sitting at a corner table by the railing, and no one seemed to notice her in the shadows. The light fixture in the vines above her was one of those which hadn't yet received its bulb, and the lemon tree in its tub beside her helped to screen her from view. She didn't want to talk to anyone, not even to Marija who looked more like a duchess than ever in her black dress with its white lace collar and cuffs. This was a good chance to mingle with all these old friends of Viktor's, to go on learning more Serbo-Croatian with much help and indulgent interest from everyone, to watch and to listen with her usual eagerness. But she sat still, her hands clasped loosely on the table in front of her, her grey eyes blank and without life.

It was some time before she noticed that Anne and Viktor were no longer of the dwindling company, and that the remaining guests were showing signs of departure. It had been a good wedding party, with plenty to eat and drink, plenty of music and singing and dancing, and now quietness was falling again over Srebro Kara. Simon came out of the house, and as he reached her, Rowena saw that he was carrying a covered basket and that he changed into slacks and a windcheater.

'No, this is not for us,' he said as he put the basket on the ground. 'Our supper or breakfast or whatever you wish to call it, is already in the jeep. This is for Milos Nimani who could not be here today, and who is so old a friend of Viktor's.'

91

'The man who lives in that little house a couple of miles away? He's paralysed or something, isn't he?'

'He was shot in the back as he knelt beside the grave he and some others had just dug for themselves. A band of partisans arrived very soon after, and Milos was one of three taken alive from the pit. The other two recovered, but Milos has had to lie on his back ever since. His – his wife and two daughters and his son all died with my own family on the same day. But he seems contented enough with his present life, and he would love to meet Anne's daughter.'

'It's not too late? Right, I'll go and change now. His house is on our way, and we won't want to come back here.'

'I have rugs in the jeep,' Simon said as she stood up, 'but you must wear all your warm clothes. That is a *very* pretty dress, but in anything like that, you would freeze to death at the top of Lovćen at dawn!'

Rowena had already taken slacks and jerseys and a borrowed parka of Viktor's down to the small sitting-room. The newly-weds couldn't go away, but at least they wouldn't be disturbed by people tramping around the top floor at all hours of the night.

The 'child who ran away from school' was much in evidence as Rowena ran a comb through her hair, picked up the parka, and went out to the hall. Family friends had already washed up and cleared away the evidence of a good party, and Marija was turning off lights and shutting doors. Rowena explained in German where she and Simon were going, and Marija's green eyes opened wide.

'Do not catch cold,' was all she said, but her smile and nod held satisfaction as she closed the front door behind them.

Milos Nimani lived with his sister Ivanka, and the Disabled War Veterans' organisation looked after them, but Ivanka made beautiful lace which added a bit to their income. Milos was wide awake when Rowena and Simon went in, and they saw that he had a book propped on a metal contrivance which could also turn the pages for him. He was delighted to see them, and his smile widened as he saw the delicacies and the bottle which Simon took from the basket. He had no English, and he spoke German only when he had to, so Rowena had to depend on Simon to interpret for them.

The room was small but bright, furnished with local woodwork and rugs, and the one incongruous object was a square box with a buzzer on it which was attached to the wall by Milos' couch. There was a telephone also on a table nearby, unusual enough in a tiny house like this, but it was the box which fascinated Rowena. She didn't like to ask about it, but she knew very well that Simon had noticed her interest and that he didn't want to satisfy it. Well, it was none of her business, and maybe she would find out about it sometime. Sometime. She suddenly remembered that now that Anne was married, there was nothing to keep her there, and that she should be seeing about her flight home any day.

It was already much colder when she and Simon left the house, and although the jeep was wonderful for country roads, it left a lot to be desired as far as warmth was concerned on a cold night. But with a rug wrapped all round her, and the hood of her parka turned up, she found that it was no hardship to withstand the night breezes.

The mountains were dark against a lighter sky where stars glittered like jewels on a velvet robe, and when at last the start of the twenty-five serpentine bends was reached, Rowena found herself sitting forward in hushed expectancy.

Simon laughed softly. 'Nothing will happen yet, and the gods have been kind and given us a clear sky. I am glad we have done this – it is like setting off into the unknown, and wondering with excitement what is to be found around the next corner. Are you warm enough?'

'Lovely. Oh, Simon, I shall never forget this as long as I live. Yes, I know, we haven't even got the sunrise yet, but I never realised how much one could see even with a little half-moon like that.'

Simon drove on, up the mountain road, the sky changing now to mauve and the stars hiding their brilliance against it. 'We will stop on this corner, I think, because then we shall have the sun come up beyond that peak.'

They both got out and sat on a low wall bordering the road just as the sun blazed up over the mountain, and spilled golden light across the rocks, the hills, the valleys. It was like a new creation, and they watched, breathless, as the sun rose higher and the waters of the fiord far below came to life in blue and gold and silver. They were so high up that they could look across the intervening hills to the Adriatic beyond Tivat, and Rowena shivered, partly with cold and partly with sheer inability to believe that what she was seeing was true.

Simon wrapped the rug around her more closely, pulled her back against him, and so they stayed, immobile, just looking, as if they could never see and remember enough of that morning. The birds were singing all around them, and smoke was beginning to rise from some of the villages before they moved.

'We cannot remain here for ever,' Simon said with a sigh. 'Perhaps it is as well that we do not live on a mountain top where we could see this every morning!

'Maybe we'd get used to it. No, we never would, because it would be different every morning, little clouds and big clouds, all pink and blue with their edges on fire.' She paused with a catch of her breath, and the loveliness below and ahead of her blurred in the bright light.

'Stay with us for a while,' Simon said suddenly, as if he knew what she had been thinking about. 'Your visa is for three months, you have given up your job, and there is no other work waiting?'

'No.'

'Then do not leave until the summer is over. You and Marija can do the Reception between you – and you can also make beds and wash dishes! These are great inducements!'

He was sitting behind her, and she couldn't see his face, and although there was laughter in his voice, she felt the tension in the shoulders she was leaning against.

'There's Keith,' she said at last. 'He's expecting me back any day now. And there's the house . . .'

'It will fall down if you do not return now?' he asked, and she giggled suddenly and light-heartedly.

'It's a beautiful, solid old house, and I love it, and a certain Mrs. Waring goes in every day to keep it in order. She certainly wouldn't mind doing that for – for another few weeks.'

'So, there remains Keith. He has his mother to look after him? You will belong to him altogether within a few months, and I think he will not bring you back here. You would not come alone?'

'I might,' Rowena said uneasily. 'It's quite likely I'd come on a flying visit now and again, just to see Mother and – and everyone else. But I don't care for the idea of separate holidays, and when one is married, there's a limit to the number of times one can rush off alone like that.'

'Naturally. So, now that you are here, it is sense to remain a little longer? If you returned now, would Keith expect to see you every day?'

'Heavens, no! He sometimes has to work odd hours in the television studios, but we usually dine out and go to the theatre or cinema once a week. And there's a meeting of our peace society once a fortnight. I'll be missing lots of these if I stay away for the summer.'

'That will do no harm,' Simon said gaily. 'You will return with a fresh mind, and you will be able to carry flags with much more vigour!'

'You're laughing at this,' she said with reproach, 'but you, of all people, should know how very terrible another war would be.'

'Ah yes, but good intentions and pure-minded protests are not enough. You forget the oppressor who was born so, and who cannot change, and who, if you offer him the other cheek, will merely place his foot upon your neck. You said to Viktor the other night that if war came, you would refuse to fight, and that there were millions like you. This I cannot believe. The good God gave to mankind the eyes to see the difference between right and wrong, He gave him the ability to choose, and the heart to fight against evil. He Himself did not hesitate to drive the wicked ones from the Temple with a whip.'

He went to the jeep for the food basket, and then returned to sit on the wall and pour coffee from the thermos. Rowena turned round in her enveloping rug and stared at him.

'But everyone in war thinks that God is on their side!' she exclaimed. 'The Germans thought that!'

'Of course,' he said evenly, 'and the tragedy of many of them is that they still think so. But that is what I meant by the ability to choose. It – it is immoral to do otherwise, immoral to believe that human nature everywhere is as perfect as your own, and that if you offer no resistance, evil will merely disappear. Do you not believe that there is a God?'

Rowena swallowed her coffee with a sense of unreality, and then gazed down at the fiord below. 'On a morning like this, I'm inclined to believe there must be Something, but I have no particular faith in a particular God. You know, I'm surprised that you have, in a Communist country, I mean. I thought they didn't go much on religion.'

'We do not have it in school,' Simon said lightly, 'but there is nothing at all to stop anyone from going to the church of his choice. No one has ever asked me if I have a faith, or if I have not. It is the business of the individual.'

'One hears so much about the persecution of religion in Communist countries . . .'

'One *hears*! And one swallows it whole, merely because an interested party says that it is so! When churchmen are told to behave, it is because they have been using their religious position to influence people in their politics. During the last war, organised religion in Croatia, apart from the Serbian Orthodox Church, sided with the invaders and led the bloodiest revenge in history on the Serbs. It is not surprising that the State now keeps all religion separate from education, and politics, and public affairs. One learns by experience, although your peace society friends may not believe so.'

Rowena sighed with exasperation, and Simon just sat looking at her, one eyebrow slightly raised, and an odd, half-amused expression in his dark eyes. Suddenly, she laughed, and the sound seemed to echo down the mountain in little bouncing trills.

'There was I,' she managed at last, 'coming to see the dawn, full of poetic thoughts and romantic dreams of beauty. And what did I get? Moral theology, politics, and constitutional law!'

Simon threw out his hands in a gesture of self-derision. 'I can only plead that this mountain air has gone to my head. It is not often that I get the chance to talk so much, and up here, there is no place for my audience to run to! But – you will think about staying with us for a while? If I promise not to argue with you any more?'

She returned his smile. 'I've thought about it, and if Viktor doesn't mind, I'd love to stay on. As you said, it's plain sense to make the most of this now that I'm here anyway. Maybe we'd better be starting back before you fall asleep over the wheel! Are you very tired?'

'Not in the least,' he said happily as he picked up the rugs and basket. 'We can sleep when we get back, but there is a kafana down in Kotor which will be open now, and we can have a wash and perhaps some more coffee.'

They didn't say much on the way down. Simon had to concentrate on his driving, and Rowena was watching the countryside with deep content. Somehow it all looked different now that she knew she wouldn't be leaving it within a few days. There was none of that desperate striving to imprint everything on the memory, that desire to stop time so that poignant moments needn't be lost for ever in the past.

'You saw the Cathedral last time?' Simon asked as they went through the West Gate leading on to the main quay. 'Twelfth century, and so beautiful. But over there in a corner of the square is perhaps something that you did not see. There are many old inscriptions and carvings, and some day I must find out where they came from – that is, if anybody knows!'

They walked over to what looked like a small garden where the ancient stones were laid out. 'This one I like so much,' Simon said, pointing. 'I wonder often who was supposed to have said it, and when.'

The inscription read: *Pax tibi, Marce, evangelista meus.*

'*Peace be unto thee,*' Rowena translated, '*Mark, my evangelist.* Yes, it does sound lovely. Doesn't that winged lion mean anything?'

'It is the symbol of Venice and of St. Mark, so it must at least date back to Venetian times. But where it came from, or who said it . . . ah well, let us go and find some

98

warm water and hot coffee. I should have shaved before we left last night – will you be seen in my company?'

Rowena looked up into the faintly rueful face, studied the shadow on his cheeks and jawline, and let her gaze linger on the network of lines at the corners of his eyes. 'I'll be seen with you anywhere, at any time. Come along Simon, amicus meus! That *is* Latin for "friend," isn't it? It never was my best subject!'

She turned quickly to walk across the square, but not before she had seen the glow in his eyes. Now what in heaven's name, she asked herself, made me say that? But it was true, so there was no harm in saying it.

Miraculously, there was hot water in the ladies' room of the kafana, and as Rowena looked in the mirror at her ruffled hair and bright eyes, she thought that no one had ever looked less like having missed a night's sleep. Somewhere up on Lovčen, she had shed a burden; she had decided to stay in Yugoslavia for a while, and the weeks stretched ahead of her, busy, rewarding, endless.

It was after eight o'clock when they got back to Srebro Kara, because they had had to wait a long time for the ferry at Kamenari. But Rowena was learning to accept things like ferries and buses that rarely ran to time, and sometimes didn't run at all, and she and Simon were laughing over her attempted conversation in Serbo-Croatian when they entered the house. Viktor and Anne were just coming downstairs, and they stopped and surveyed the newcomers with amusement.

'*What* a couple of scarecrows!' Anne exclaimed. 'But you look as if you've had a wonderful time.'

'We had,' Rowena said fervently, and then looked at Viktor. 'Would you mind awfully if I didn't go back to England yet? I wouldn't be in the way – I mean, I'd help at the desk, and keep your books, and do the bedrooms, and—'

'Stop!' He held up his hand, and came to the foot of the stairs and hugged her. 'Dear child, we would love to keep you even if you never lifted a finger! Of course you must stay, and see how happy you have made my beautiful wife!'

Anne looked, if possible, happier than a moment before, and Simon grinned widely. 'You see?' he said to Rowena. 'I told you they would want another kitchen servant!'

They both went upstairs to catch up on some sleep, and near the top they glanced down into the hall, and stood still. Viktor and Anne had paused outside the small sitting-room, looking at each other, and there was that in their faces which made Rowena catch her breath. There was no need to wonder if those two had found all they had ever wanted in their 'end of the journey and the beginning of all delight.'

Beside her, Simon stood motionless, his face grave and his eyes shadowed, so very different from his mirthful expression of a few moments before. She touched his arm gently and went on to her own room, knowing that he was thinking of Natalya, and of the wasted months that might elapse before they could get married too.

When she wakened in the middle of the afternoon, Rowena washed and dressed and got out her writing-case. Keith had to be told that she wouldn't be home until perhaps the end of the summer, and after she had rejected all her rather anxious explanations, she decided that the plain fact of her staying on must be enough for him. There was nothing unreasonable in her wishing to stay for a time with the mother who would soon be left more than a thousand miles away.

Somewhat to everyone's surprise, Srebro Kara was ready for the first guests two days before they were due to arrive, and the breathing-space was especially welcome to Rowena who had seldom worked so hard in her life.

But she was enjoying herself, and her tiredness was gone when Simon suggested a walk on the night before the hotel opened. Natalya went too, and they ended up in a kafana about two miles along the road. The place was very crowded, but room was made for them at a table in one corner, and they sat drinking coffee and slivovica. As usual, a group of men were singing Montenegrin and Macedonian songs, and Rowena smiled as she watched them.

'I wish I had a tape recorder,' she said. 'I've never yet been in a local café without hearing at least half the customers burst into song for no reason at all! I'd play the tape over to myself when I'm in London, and imagine I was back here again. I'd have to have some slivovica too, but *not* Turkish coffee – I'll never get used to the stuff. Oh – there's Gunther!'

The other two followed her gaze to an opposite table where Gunther Kleist was smiling at her through the haze of tobacco smoke, and as Natalya moved along, he came to join them. Rowena introduced them, and was suddenly startled to feel tension in Simon's arm which was close to her own.

'I thought you were all leaving soon after Keith,' she said to Gunther. 'Are you on your own?'

'From today, yes, but my mother may join me soon. Willi and Marta went away yesterday, but I do not mind being left. It is interesting to come to places like this, and to listen to the singing, and to take life easily. You may recall that Willi was always wishing to be on the move!'

Rowena laughed. 'He made me tired to look at him!'

'Ah,' Simon murmured. 'You are the friends with whom Rowena and Keith went touring. You will be staying on for some time?'

'I have no plans,' Gunther said vaguely. 'I have my car here, and if my mother flies down from Bonn, we may tour some more of the country. She knows this coast well –

her family came for holidays every year when she was a girl.'

Simon nodded. 'One understands why so many Germans preferred the Adriatic to the North Sea or the Baltic! But even so, they have always come here in much greater numbers than the British or the Belgians or the Dutch. It is strange.'

'I do not think so,' Gunther said with a shrug. 'Under the Austrian Empire, you had to speak much German here, and it was useful for us to come to a place where our language was known. That is why we have always felt at home in this country.'

His gaze wandered away to a couple who had just come in, and he didn't notice that his words had dropped into a little pool of silence. Even Rowena, who hadn't lived through it, was thinking of the torture and carnage the Germans had brought to this country in which they felt so much 'at home.' But, Rowena told herself quickly, Gunther was the new generation, and it was more than likely that he had never heard of the German record of brutality in Yugoslavia. The Almighty could talk of visiting the sins of the fathers on the children, but ordinary human beings couldn't see it in quite the same light. If they did, all life would become the senseless, murderous vandettas practised by the Corsicans for endless generations.

When they started to walk along the homeward road, Natalya looked at Simon in the starlight. 'You did not like him,' she said, and it was a flat statement. 'He was quite good-looking, he was pleasant, and he was interested in our customs. I could see no outward reasons for dislike. So?'

He said nothing, and they walked along in silence for a while. At last, Rowena put a tentative hand on his arm. 'Simon? Gunther is only about twenty – he wasn't born

102

when this country was occupied. You – you're not *blaming* him for anything are you?'

'No,' Simon said on an explosive sigh. 'But he is one of the cold ones. They frighten me, so little do the generations change their racial characteristics. This young Kleist would be one of those so ready to lift the fallen torch of his fathers. It would not matter to him that it was a dead torch, a shameful brand which had lit so many funeral pyres. As long as it was a *German* torch, he would carry it with a terrible and single-minded pride. Oh no, I am not blaming him for what his people did here, but I shudder at his likeness to those who went before him.'

He spoke with conviction and with sadness, and there was nothing that the two girls could say. Natalya's childhood, under Italian occupation, had been hard but not grim, and Rowena had known nothing at all of war or its horrors. She had strong views and strong prejudices, but when she came up against bitter experience, she found that she had no answers to give.

The first guests arrived at the hotel the following day, and by dinner time there were fifteen people sitting at the tables in the vinery. Anne, Natalya, and Marija worked in the kitchen, while Viktor, Simon and Rowena waited at the tables. It would become necessary later on to employ more labour, but for the moment they had to learn by experience just how much work they could share between them all without undue fatigue. Anne had had the forethought to supply herself with white nylon overalls, and because of the button-through style and pleated skirts, they fitted the other three women fairly well too.

'We're going to manage beautifully,' Rowena said with an appraising glance round the kitchen later that night. 'Funny how easy it is to wash up when there's plenty of space and four women to do it! And the guests are rather pleasant, don't you think? They've all been to the Dalmatian coast before, but they seem to think that this is the nicest place they've ever stayed in. Hooray for us!'

Viktor kissed her on the cheek as he passed with a tray of glasses and bottles of slivovica. 'And especially for you, darling! I am quite sure they have never seen so pretty or so enthusiastic a waitress at any table! Stay with us – become one of the family – you will be so good for business!'.

His words were light, but his brown eyes were serious as he looked down at her, and Rowena flushed as she shook her head. 'I'm only a stop-gap, Viktor, filling in time for selfish reasons. Don't try to tempt me away from my own plans.'

'No, I should not do that. Forgive me, my almost-daughter, for trying to keep hold of you. We are all selfish when it comes to our own desires, and we do not look forward to the day when you will leave us for ever.'

She looked after the big figure in the white jacket and dark trousers, and caught her lower lip hard between her teeth. James Fairfax had never been much of a father to her, and she had seemed to manage well enough without him. But Viktor Petrović – ah, that was different. The love of father and daughter had sprung to life, full-grown, between them, and it was something they had both longed for, however unconsciously.

Anne came over to her and they went out to the hall together. 'Don't worry about him,' Anne said with her rare intuition. 'It's not every man who has as nice an adopted son as Simon, and it's asking too much of the gods to add a daughter as well!'

'Not when the daughter wants it too,' Rowena said rather unsteadily, and her mother looked at her with concern.

'Then you'll have to come back as often as possible,' she said firmly. 'I know Keith doesn't care for us or for this country, but it's quite ridiculous for us all to take it for granted – as we have been doing – that because of that, you won't be coming back. You're not exactly a wealthy woman, but your father left you quite enough money for you to indulge in some extravagances. You've called yourself a progressive modern often enough, heaven knows, so *be* progressive enough to fly out here by yourself at least two or three times a year.'

She was silent for a few moments, frowning. 'You know, you're the last person I would have pictured as being so deferential to the wishes of a husband. What brought it on?'

'I suppose it started that day in Dubrovnik, when Keith and I almost quarrelled about the place. It really was my fault. I irritated him by being a bit of a smug know-all about everything Yugoslav. Maybe my subconscious has been trying to make amends ever since, by deciding that Keith and I will keep off the subject altogether! I wonder how he'll reply to my letter? If he's very disappointed, I shall feel so awful, and so guilty, although I know I shouldn't.'

Keith's answer arrived a few days later, and it was so sweet and understanding that Rowena re-read it with a wide smile and a sigh of relief. Of course he would miss her, he said, but she was quite right to stay where she was until her visa expired. He hadn't realised how much she wanted to stay with her mother for a while . . . it had poured in London all week, and she was much better off where she was . . . the wedding had sounded such fun, and he really did wish he'd been there . . . he was glad that Anne and Viktor were so happy, and he sent Anne his love and warmest wishes.

'Good news?' Simon asked lightly as he stood beside her. They had been clearing the lunch tables when the letters came, and Rowena had dropped to a chair in the vinery.

'Lovely,' she said. 'Keith can just about manage to

do without me until my visa expires! He was on my conscience a bit, but, bless his heart, he's made everything so easy for me.'

They both looked towards the front gate when they heard a car draw up, and they moved forward as the driver jumped out. He was wearing khaki bush-jacket and shorts, his skin was deeply bronze, and he was looking at the façade of the house with a delighted smile.

'Oh, no,' Rowena said in a hollow voice. 'The Poona major in person! It's Uncle Oliver – Mother's uncle – guaranteed to set any group of people by the ears within ten minutes!'

7

SIMON looked at Oliver Stanwick with some amusement, and said to Rowena: 'He does not look so very formidable! Is this not the man who fought in Serbia in both wars? Viktor will be *so* delighted to meet him – we owe much to men like that.'

Wars again, Rowena thought impatiently. As if Oliver and Viktor and Simon hadn't had enough horror to last them a lifetime! Now battles would be re-fought at every meal, with cutlery and condiments to mark positions and brigades and divisions.

Anne came running through the front doorway, plainly delighted to see her uncle, and when Viktor was introduced, the two men studied each other and then grinned as they shook hands. Rowena followed Simon to join the group, and although she wasn't at all pleased to see Oliver, it was a shock to find that he was even less pleased to see her.

'Thought you'd have gone home by now,' he said gruffly. 'Young Manning here too?'

'He's gone back,' Anne said, with her usual swift smoothing of ruffled feelings between her daughter and her uncle. 'Well, this is a lovely surprise. I had no idea you'd left England.'

Oliver seemed a little sheepish as he glanced back towards his Land Rover, and when everyone else looked at it too, they saw what seemed to be a pile of sacking in the back.

'Had to bring you a wedding present,' he said, 'and I

wanted it to be something special. Plenty silver back in Pimlico, and I'm sure you can send for it if you want it. But – I don't know – how much spare ground have you?'

'Spare ground?' Anne echoed faintly. 'What *have* you got? There's a lovely stretch of green beyond the vinery, and it runs back into trees and then a boundary wall. And there's a field with little stables where we keep our five donkeys, but . . .'

'Well, see what you think anyway. I was going to call on you first, to see what might be appropriate, and then I stayed last week with a friend down in Macedonia. The minute I saw it – this – I thought to myself: "That's for Anne." My friend thought I was mad, but you won't. Go along on to the grass and wait a minute. Viktor, if you'd give a hand?'

'It just couldn't be a crocodile,' Rowena muttered as she strolled with Simon along the side of the house. 'They don't have them in Macedonia, do they? Or apes? Or bears?'

'I will take you to meet a bear any day you please,' Simon said cheerfully. 'We have plenty of them up in the mountains. But Uncle Oliver would have more sense of fitness than to bring any of these things. He loves Anne, and he wishes to give her pleasure.'

Rowena saw her mother put her hands up to her face, and then kneel on the grass with an exclamation of joy. There came a delicate tip-tapping along the path, a tiny donkey came into view, and it went straight to Anne and put its head on her shoulder. Rowena had never seen such a shade before – Siamese-cat-colour, she thought – and she had never seen such a small animal away from its mother.

'He's fully-grown,' Oliver said, as he looked down at his neice who was entranced with her present. 'I couldn't believe it myself, but it's a fact. If my friend had known the phrase about bringing coals to Newcastle, he'd have

108

used it! Said you'd be bound to have donkeys here already, but I knew you wouldn't have one like this. Nice little chap.'

'Oh, darling,' Anne said to Viktor, 'will he be all right with the bigger ones in the field?'

He laughed, and placed a hand on her shoulder. 'They will all take turns to make a fuss of him! But I have an idea that this is the one who will end up in the garden! They all love human company, but I think this lad will insist on it – *and* he'll get it, and have more admirers than any film star!'

'That's all right then,' Oliver said contentedly. 'I've been calling him George on the journey, but if you can think of anything better, I don't suppose he'll mind! As he's a Yugoslav donkey, maybe it had better be Djordje, which sounds the same anyway.' He grinned at Viktor. 'I often used to take Anne to the Zoo, even when she was a grown woman. Couldn't get her away from the darn' donkeys, ever!'

Anne rose to her feet and kissed him. 'I remember. It was a lovely thought to bring an extra special one like Djordje. Let's go and introduce him to the others.'

Rowena left them to it, and went to help Natalya and Marija in the kitchen. She knew she was being unreasonable and petty, but Uncle Oliver had always annoyed her, and she resented the fact that Simon had been so quick to credit him with good points which he couldn't possibly know he possessed. It was unfortunate, but Uncle Oliver always brought out the worst in her; he made her feel tight-lipped and disapproving, which she was, but she hated not being able to hide it.

The family usually had dinner when they could fit it in between serving the guests, but that night they waited until they could all sit down together in their private sitting-room. Oliver had refused to stay in the house, saying firmly that he had already made arrangements further along the coast, and that he had had no intention of landing on Srebro Kara unannounced. But he would be in the area for a week or two, and he intended to drop in from time to time.

He thanked Viktor for the invitation, and added: 'You forget that I have lots of very old friends scattered all over this country. You've no idea the kick I get out of maybe leaning over a wall until the chap I'm waiting for turns round and sees me. He stares for a second, and then throws his arms wide and yells: "Oleever!" and it's usually a race to see who gets over the wall first!'

'I know,' Anne said reminiscently. 'I met my old boss recently, and although I was dying to have news of Viktor from him, I took time to be thrilled to bits at just seeing him again.'

Viktor mentioned Oliver's service in eastern Bosnia, but the older man changed the subject, and he did the same whenever the talk seemed to drift towards either war. Viktor was a bit puzzled, but Simon and Anne weren't, and Rowena simmered with irritation because Oliver was refusing to mention his favourite subject while she was around. She didn't take coffee at the end of the meal, and rose to get Simon's silver tray.

'I'll see to the drinks outside,' she said briefly, and went to take orders from the people who were sitting at the cleared tables in the vinery. It kept her busy, and she was able to give Oliver a casual wave when he left, and to go on giving change to a couple at a corner table. Some time later, Viktor took over, and she wandered out to the hall where Marija was sitting knitting behind the reception desk.

'Are you managing all right?' Rowena asked, and Marija beamed at her.

'All questions I have been able to answer,' she said, 'and I begin to understand about passports and about the

110

forms which are to be filled in. It was so good of you to think of me for this job, and to tell Viktor who might not have thought of it. I like to do bedrooms in the mornings, but here one meets everybody, and it is so interesting, and also they treat me like a schoolmistress who is to be much respected!'

'Duchess,' Rowena said affectionately, 'you put them in their place with just one flick of your eyelashes. You and the beautiful new donkey – my goodness, we're getting to be quite the showplace of the Adriatic!'

She felt less at odds with the world as she left Marija chuckling at the desk, and she went upstairs to change out of her overall and pick up a woolly. It was a beautiful calm night, and she strolled along above the beach, listening to the lapping of the water among the stones. She didn't want to think about anything in particular, and she didn't mind one way or the other when Simon caught up with her and they walked along together.

'How far?' he asked when they had gone about a mile. 'You rise so early these days, and it will not do if you return to England too tired to move!'

'Oh, but the mornings are so beautiful that it's a crime to waste them. Anyway, I'm used to walking, and I find it relaxing after a hard day's work. Let's just go as far as the tourist camp – I can hear music.'

But when they drew nearer, they found that the music was 'canned', and that several radios were tuned to different stations. None of them were over-loud, but the road passed close to the camp boundary, and each tent had its devotee of classics or folksong or light music.

'No fiddles or guitars,' Rowena said ruefully. 'I thought there might have been a sing-song in progress, but I'd forgotten that all these people are "foreigners," and not so likely to burst into song as you lot! Oh well, let's go back and—'

111

She broke off with a gasp, and at the same moment Simon saw the Land Rover with its small tent beside it.

'Now why does he have to go and do something like this!' Rowena exclaimed crossly. 'A tourist camp is no place for him! I've a good mind to root him out and take him back with us to a proper bed!'

'You will leave him alone,' Simon insisted. 'Why will you permit pride to most people, but none at all to your Uncle Oliver? He had never met Viktor, he could have embarrassed your mother by appearing so suddenly, and it could have seemed that he was making use of her connection with a hotel. And, tomorrow, you will *not* mention where he spent the night!'

Rowena looked at him in surprise, and then turned and started to walk back with him towards Srebro Kara. 'I – I didn't think about his pride. He's such an old fire-eater that I suppose I never credit him with any sensitivity at all. *You've* never heard him talk for hours on end about his precious army, and about all the glorious, gory battles he's had the pleasure of fighting!'

'Neither have you,' Simon said with assurance. 'You may have heard a few memories from a man who had an interesting life, and who did his duty well, but he would never *dare* to speak for hours in front of your accusing eyes! Knowing that you saw him as one who delighted in murder and barbarity and horror, he would dry up as a squeezed sponge!'

'But he *enjoyed* his wars! He's said so often!'

'So? Most people did. I did.'

'Simon!'

'I am not talking about the tragic ones who were tortured and imprisoned or who died in agony. But danger forges a bond between men who are fighting for the same cause; a friend's life becomes more precious than your own; you are surrounded by a warmth, a – a fellow-

112

feeling, the wish to share in every experience whether it is good or bad. When the danger is over, those who are still alive go home, and oh, so often you wonder where all that warmth and kindness and comradeship has gone.'

Rowena shook her head in disbelief. 'I think that's quite dreadful. You're as good as saying that wars are inevitable because mankind really enjoys them, that happy memories of shared danger are worth all the horrors that went with them.'

'I said nothing like that,' Simon said patiently. 'I know that news of another war now would cause Oliver and Viktor and myself to grieve almost beyond bearing. But once we were involved, I have no doubt that we would find that same comradeship which we knew before. Dear Rowena, you are closing your mind to the workings of the human heart, to the nature of human beings. You are so obsessed by your dread of war that you proclaim that everything connected with it is evil, and with all the evil you throw away also the justice, the integrity, the courage, and the matchless triumph of the human spirit.'

'But – the people who had those things – surely they don't lose them as soon as peace returns.'

They slowed down within sight of Srebro Kara, and Simon took her hand. 'No, but their influence is limited once they return to their own private lives. It is a sad fact which we cannot ignore, that it is danger and disaster on a large scale which release the world's compassion and make every man a brother. You remember our dreadful earthquake in Skopje a few years ago? One of your famous television commentators appeared on your screens on the day it happened, and he said, quite simply; 'I am asking you for a hundred thousand pounds'. He told about Skopje, and in three days he had a million pounds. Viktor and I could not speak when we heard of it.' He

113

smiled a little. 'We went to church, and found many others giving thanks for the same thing.'

Rowena was silent until they entered the hall where Marija was just leaving her post. They said good night to her, and went on to the kitchen to make hot chocolate.

'You're too clever for me,' Rowena said at last. 'I can't reason as you can, so maybe it's just my instincts that make me a pacifist at heart.'

Simon grinned at her. 'But you will not accept that Oliver and I are also pacifists at heart? You see, the very thought shocks you! But it is true, and if you will search your conscience you will have to admit that it is so.'

'My instincts would keep me from fighting. Yours never would.'

'That would be insanity rather than pacifism!'

Natalya came in with Anne, and they looked with resignation from Simon to Rowena.

'They are on politics again,' Natalya murmured. 'One would think there must be other things in the world, no? It will be terrible for them both when one will convert the other, or when the one will go away and there will be no one with whom to argue. I am sad for them, as you also must be.'

'Shattered,' Anne agreed with a laugh, 'but no doubt it's good for them both to meet the opposition! Simon, angel, it's your turn to wait for the last of the guests to take themselves off to bed. And do make sure that Frau Hersher isn't mooning on the beach before you shut the big doors!'

Rowena was smiling as she went upstairs with her mother. Frau Hersher was a rather woolly-minded old dear, and her idea of bliss was to sit on the shore under the stars and recite to herself the poems of Goethe and Heine. Before the family had become aware of this, Viktor had left her out one night, and then by good fortune he had seen her from his bedroom window, and rushed out to get her.

In her own room, Rowena sat on the bed and looked up at the ikon of the Angel of Mileševo, thinking of all she and Simon had discussed, and remembering Natalya's remark that soon there would be no one with whom to argue. But it wasn't the arguments that mattered, it was the meeting of minds, the exploration of new byways along roads considered to be well-known and well-trodden. She took a last look at the Angel, and she put out the light, laughing a little at herself because she was so oddly enjoying what she had once called Simon's lectures on moral theology, politics and constitutional law.

A few evenings later, she was waiting at tables when she hesitated over a German phrase.

'It is all right,' said Fraulein Einhardt who was sitting alone, 'we will speak English. Are you on a working vacation?'

'Oh, no, not really. I know the people who run the hotel, and I'm just helping out at the busy periods. I can see I'll have to brush-up on my schoolgirl German!'

'Yes,' Fraulein Einhardt agreed seriously, 'it is the language most useful and necessary to know in Europe now, and in particular if you stay long in Yugoslavia.'

'I'm learning Serbo-Croatian, which should be even more useful, don't you think? It's odd, but I'm not finding it as difficult as I thought I would. Have you ever tried it?'

'Never. There was no need, and I have been coming to this country for seven years. These Slav languages are barbaric.' She paused, and her gaze followed Natalya who had come out by the service door and gone to speak to Viktor at the cutlery table. 'Who is that? I have not seen her before.'

Rowena's eyebrows rose at the sharpness in the woman's tone. 'She's the cook, and a friend of the family.'

'Strange. I have not seen one of them here before. She is, of course, a Jew?'

The question so took Rowena's breath away, that for a moment she didn't know what to say. What could it matter to this creature with the light blue eyes if the cook was a Hottentot and looked equally pretty in a white overall?

'I don't know what she is,' Rowena said at last in an even voice. 'The – ah, Nazis did away with almost eighty thousand Yugoslav Jews during the war, so maybe our cook is one of the remaining six thousand or so. Would you like me to ask her?'

Fury glittered in the pale eyes as Fraulein Einhardt looked Rowena up and down, but Rowena made herself stand there with a polite smile of enquiry on her face.

'I would *not* like you to ask her,' Fraulein Einhardt snapped. 'You are insolent!'

'I beg your pardon for upsetting you,' Rowena murmured, and walked away with her trayful of crockery which she dumped on the kitchen table with a small crash. Viktor had followed her in, and he put a hand on her shoulder.

'Is something wrong?' he asked, and she looked from him to Oliver while she told what had been said.

'I'm very sorry I was rude to one of your guests, Viktor,' she finished, 'because she was mad enough to walk out there and then. I apologised for upsetting her, but I'm darned if I'll apologise for anything I said to her! She's just the type who might complain higher up, and make things difficult for you.'

'She would not get far,' Viktor comforted her. 'The kind of remark she made to you is – oddly enough! – not popular in this country. I doubt that she will walk out, but I assure you that I would not mind if she does. You spoke quite rightly in answer to her, so think no more about it.'

Oliver put down the silver he was cleaning. 'Would

she be the middle-aged one who's about as broad as she's long? The one who knows everything? Yes, a typical Hun, that one. She tried to tell Marija a thing or two today, but the duchess just looked at her, and the Einhardt scuttled off like a dachshund down a hole!' He grinned at Rowena. 'You've got the same snooty look as the duchess sometimes – try it on Einhardt next time you come across her.'

'I might, at that,' Rowena said, a little awed by the light of approval in Oliver's far-seeing eyes. It was the first time in her adult life that she could recall having seen such a thing.

Later that night, she joined Marija at the reception desk for their mutual lessons in English and Serbo-Croatian. Their methods may not have been educationally scientific, but they were getting on very well, and their absorbed interest made up for many shortcomings. Oliver, on his way back to his 'hotel', stopped beside them for a few moments, and Viktor joined him in testing Rowena's progress.

'Not bad,' Oliver admitted, and then he sighed. 'When we're both back in England, we'll have to meet now and again just to keep the language green. Cousin Hilda has a picture in her mind of "the Balkans" that dates from the turn of the century, and I daren't mention "that savage place" at home.'

The telephone rang, and after listening for a second, Marija thrust the receiver at Viktor. 'Milos Nimani,' she whispered. 'He says to find you at once!'

Rowena stared as Viktor's face seemed to go suddenly haggard, and then he nodded to Marija who hurried to the family sitting-room. Viktor's rapid conversation with Milos was soon over, and when he replaced the receiver, he turned to look at Simon and Anne and Natalya who had come running out with Marija.

117

'It has come at last,' Viktor said. 'I could hear the alarm ringing while Milos was speaking. Simon – hurry!'

Simon raced upstairs, and Anne gripped Viktor's arms. 'You won't be armed, will you? Promise me you'll stay out of trouble!'

'I promise, my darling. No guns, nothing at all.'

'We'll take my car,' Oliver said, as he went to the door. 'It's just outside, and as good as the jeep for that narrow track.'

'What's going *on*?' Rowena demanded, as Simon appeared with jackets and a magnificent flashlight camera. 'You all seem to know about it but me!'

'Come and find out,' Simon said, and tossed her a spare parka. His skin had a strange pallor under the tan, so that he looked pinched and yellow. 'It is all right, Anne, I promise she will come to no harm. The man we go to meet will not have shared his secret, and he is not in a position to defend himself now.'

Completely puzzled, but caught up in the prevailing tension, Rowena took a last look at her mother's doubtful expression and at Natalya's oddly bored one, and then ran after the three men. Viktor sat with Oliver, and Rowena got in behind with Simon who had placed the camera carefully between his feet.

'This goes back to the death of my village,' he said, and hugged himself as if he were suddenly cold. 'It was almost over when a motor-cyclist brought some alarm or other to the Germans – probably that partisans were rumoured to be nearby. The Colonel in charge of the – the operation ordered his men to leave, including the driver of his own small car, and then he took a metal box from the front seat. I had seen soldiers go to the car quite often, and once the sun had glinted on the wedding rings and other jewellery one had poured from his hand.'

Rowena tucked her hand through his arm, and leaned on

118

his shoulder in wordless sympathy. What could one *say* about an inhumanity which murdered and burned defenceless villagers, and never forgot to remove the trinkets of gold and silver?

'The Colonel also had a spade,' Simon went on, 'and he passed underneath the branches where I was hiding. I did not realise then that my terror had almost welded me to that tree, and I felt sick at the thought of falling down right in front of that monster. He was in a hurry, but he chose his spot well. There were small boulders all through the wood, and he overturned one which ended in a peaked top which could be gripped. He dug a hole underneath, put in his box which seemed very heavy, and then he replaced the boulder. He smoothed the ground nearby, and then got into his car and drove after his men.'

The Land Rover turned off the main road, and Viktor turned to look at Rowena.

'Simon was very shocked after his experience,' he said, 'and it was some time before he remembered the buried box and told us about it. We got it out, and it was full of what must have been that Colonel's entire haul of gold and silver and jewellery in Yugoslavia. Some of it was traced back to surviving relatives, but most of it went to help people like Milos who had lost wives and families in such incidents.'

'Milos,' Rowena said. 'I suppose that box on his wall was the alarm signal you mentioned? I wondered what it was when we called there on the night we went up Mount Lovčen.'

'The thought of tonight has been with Milos for a long time,' Viktor said soberly. 'The use of his hands and brain was all that was left to him, and because he had been an electrical engineer, he made a trap out of the metal box, and the rest of us rigged up the alarm to his directions. The authorities know, of course – that is why Milos has the telephone in that little house. We have promised to hand the criminal over without a mark on him.'

'It's been more than twenty years,' Oliver said as he slowed down. 'I wonder why he took so long to come back?'

'I stopped expecting him long ago,' Simon muttered. 'Viktor was sure he was dead, but Milos would not have it. He said the man might have been in prison as a war criminal, but we did not know his name, and could not find out. He said also that the most devilish of the killers bore charmed lives, and that when this Colonel was sure he was safe, he would return for his loot. Stop here, Oliver – the place is over there to the right.'

When the engine was switched off, the sound of the night breezes could be heard rustling through the trees, and the flashlight attachment of the camera shook as Simon got out of the car.

'All right?' Viktor asked quickly, and Simon handed over the camera, and wiped his face with his sleeve.

'Sorry, I could not hold it steady. That man's face – I have never forgotten it – he worked without his cap on, and my eyes themselves were like lenses which made photographs on my mind. Ah – there is his light.'

Rowena swallowed hard as she looked in the same direction and saw a small glow among the trees. Viktor and Oliver went first, and almost unconsciously Simon gripped Rowena's hand and followed them. They saw the boulder, then the big torch which had rolled along the ground, and then they heard the grunting and straining of someone in the darkness.

Oliver picked up the torch and directed its beam on the overturned boulder, a heap of earth, a spade, and then on the figure lying prone on the ground with hands seemingly caught fast in the freshly-dug hole.

'Help me,' the man urged in German, and as he lifted his face towards them, Rowena and Simon gasped.

'Gunther Kleist!' Rowena exclaimed, and just then the torch went out, and they all jumped as Viktor took a flashlight picture.

'Not exactly the man we expected,' Viktor said in an expressionless voice, 'but one with guilty knowledge nevertheless. Oliver, put on the torch for a moment, and clear the earth from the top of the box so that it can be clearly seen. Thank you.'

He took several photographs, and then directed the beam of his own big torch on the young German who was already twisting away from the other bright light.

'Get me out of this trap!' Gunther screamed, and then fell silent as Simon stepped forward and looked down at him.

'Where is your father?' Simon asked. 'I saw the likeness that night I met you in the kafana, but I could not believe it. Why did your father not come himself to reclaim his treasure?'

'My father is dead,' Gunther said with a sob of exhaustion in his voice. 'Please free my hands – I have done no harm! My father said part of my legacy was here – we could not understand what he meant, and I was only eleven when he died. Then this year, my mother found a map in the lining of his identity case, so – so I came to see what it was all about.'

'And you made no guesses?' Viktor asked softly. 'You saw the ruins of the village over there, and you did not ask yourself why your father should bury your – ah, legacy in this spot? In the name of heaven, what kind of creature are you?'

He bent and manipulated something at one end of the box, and Gunther freed his wrist with a gasp of relief. Viktor and Oliver pulled him to his feet, and the box came with him, still attached to his other hand by a circle of metal like a handcuff. Gunther looked dazedly at the box, and then at Viktor.

121

'Yes, it is almost empty,' Viktor told him, 'and I think we will leave it where it is for the moment. We want Milos to see how well his trap worked.'

He was thoughtful for a second, then handed the second torch to Oliver, and with a swift movement took Gunther's wallet from his breast pocket. The young man lifted his free hand, but Oliver growled in German under his breath, and hefted the torch like a club.

'I knew it,' Viktor said wearily. 'Not only did the Colonel draw a map for his son, he also told him that the value of the gold alone was worth at least two thousand marks. And he is most insistent that only mother and son know about it!' Viktor scanned the rest of the paper. 'Ah, here are some clever ways by which the treasure may be secretly taken out of the country! So, Herr Kleist, you only came here to see what it was all about? You and your mother understood nothing? But it is all written here in good, plain German!'

'You scum of the earth,' Rowena said with sick loathing. 'What your father did here was bestial, but you approved it and were willing to profit by it! I – I could kill you myself!'

She burst into tears, and Simon put an arm round her shoulder and walked back to the car with her.

8

ROWENA wept with abandon for a few moments, and then took a deep breath and found a handkerchief.

'I'm sorry,' she murmured, as she rubbed at her face. 'It's worse for you than for me. Oh, Simon, I never felt so – so vicious before. It was all I could do not to leap at him with all my claws out! He made me feel unclean, as ugly as himself.'

'I know,' Simon said, and stroked her hair gently, 'but you were just being very human, very full of human anger. With him and his father, inhumanity is in the blood, like a disease. I – I do not know how I feel now. Before we saw that it was the son who was lying there, I was glad that we had promised ourselves not to bring weapons if the alarm was ever raised. When one is a little crazy with hatred and nausea, it does not do to have a gun in the hand. If it had been the Colonel waiting there – I would be ready to hand him over to justice now – but that first five minutes – I do not know – I will never know—'

She turned and took his cold hands in both of hers. 'It doesn't matter any more. It's over, and maybe now you can forget the Colonel's face and – and what you saw him do.'

The other three joined them, Gunther having to hold the box with his free hand as well, because it was too heavy to leave it dangling from the captive wrist. Viktor shone a light on a small bunch of keys which he had taken from Gunther.

'His car will be somewhere off the main road,' he said to Simon, 'but I do not think he will be using it tonight. First, we shall call on Milos. Will you drive? Oliver and I will escort this beauty. You know, I was shocked at the time, but now I really understand the people of Kragujevac.'

Rowena shivered. 'So do I. God help me, so do I.'

She got in beside Simon, recalling the story which had so horrified her when she first heard it. During the war, the Germans had made a reprisal raid on Kragujevac, shooting about seven thousand men, and machine-gunning a schoolful of children. Then, almost twenty years later, one of the Germans responsible had returned to the town *on holiday*, had been recognised on the street, and lynched.

Now, remembering her own reactions to the story, she knew that her horror at the death of the tourist had been as great as her horror at what he had done. Her mind had rejected the picture of a schoolful of dead children and so many thousands of dead men, and she had even said to Simon that perhaps the poor man had returned to try to make amends. No wonder Simon had looked at her in stunned silence, and then left her.

Anne and Marija were waiting at the gate of Srebro Kara, and Simon gave them a quick explanation before driving on to the little house where the paralysed Milos lived with his sister. Gunther looked round in fear as he was hauled out of the car and made to walk indoors, and he blinked in the bright light of the room where Milos was watching with a terrible eagerness.

Viktor quickly explained what had happened, and who the trap had caught, and when he finished, Milos was staring at Gunther with slow tears running down his seamed face.

'Your father burned my wife and three children in a church,' he said in German, 'and I have waited for the day

124

when he would be brought here to me. But he has gone elsewhere for his reward, and he is surely receiving it. So, you may have your legacy. Shake the box a little – do you hear that noise? We left the gold-mounted teeth for your father, as a reminder of his busy, happy life in this country. Now you may have them, to present to your lady mother who found the map and the instructions.'

He turned his head away on the pillow, and his sister wiped his eyes and stared with cold curiosity at Gunther.

'I only wish to be rid of this box!' Gunther raged. 'Take it away from me! My mother is at the hotel – she will be out of her mind with anxiety by now!'

'I think she must be a very tough example of woman-hood,' Viktor said. 'Which is fortunate, as she will have to find some way of removing this box from your hand. You see, the spring which Milos made frees only one hand and the weight which was keeping the box in place. Someone will have to use a saw on the other – ah, bracelet.'

'No,' Gunther managed, straining at the handcuff, and seeing the redness on his wrist where he had already striven to release himself without avail. 'It is not possible!'

'Cease pulling,' Viktor advised, 'or your hand will swell, and there will be no room to use a saw. You may leave now.'

Gunther just didn't believe what was happening to him, and when he understood that he was on his own, he stammered that it was miles and miles back to his hotel. Surely they were going to return his car keys? Surely they were going to drive him to the place where his car had been left?

'Why?' Oliver asked simply, as he opened the door and pushed him outside. 'You got yourself into this mess. Now get out of it. Mind your legacy – you nearly bashed it against the fence.'

Oliver followed him out to the road, to make sure he

went on his way, and then returned to sit in the Land Rover in case Gunther got any ideas about it.

Inside, Viktor dropped to the bed and touched his old friend's shoulder. 'I must tell the police, Milos. We promised them that. But I think they will see the point of letting Kleist make his own way home, and they will let him and his mother have a few hours of anxiety before they turn up with a saw!'

Simon rubbed his chin. 'Viktor – Kleist wouldn't do anything foolish, would he?'

'Well, he's almost hysterical with fury, but his sense of self-preservation is as strong as his father's. There is no need to fear that he might walk into the sea and just keep going. No, put anything like that out of your mind.'

Viktor used the telephone, and when he was finished, Milos gave him a faint smile.

'I am glad it is all over, Viktor. I waited so long for revenge, but even if it had been the Colonel who had been caught, I do not think I would feel any different. It is like – like being washed clean. Grief for those we loved is honest and sweet, and at the last it heals, but vengeance leaves an open wound, and a man can die of that alone.'

Rowena looked at him and marvelled at the resilience of the human spirit. There he lay, paralysed and bereft, because of man's inhumanity to man, but long and painful years later he could still be glad that vengeance didn't belong to him.

On the way back to Srebro Kara, they looked for Gunther Kleist, but he must have stepped out to some purpose because he was still ahead when they went into the house. His box wasn't too heavy, but it was cumbersome, and he would want to cover the eight or nine miles to his hotel before dawn.

Anne and Marija had tea and coffee ready in the sitting-room, and Rowena was the only one who seemed surprised that Natalya had gone to bed. But she had noticed before that any mention of the war years bored Natalya, and now she was shocked because the girl couldn't be bothered to wait up for the man she loved.

'Gunther,' Anne was saying, after she had heard the story from Viktor. 'Yes, I'm not surprised. On the night I dined with the six of them, when Keith was there, I found them quite terrifying in their assurance of righteousness. Willi wasn't so bad – his sense of humour was his salvation – but he was the exception in that little party.'

'Monsters,' Rowena said bitterly, 'all of them. I swear I've never been race or colour or creed-conscious all my life, but in what category can Germans be put anyway?'

'In that of human beings,' Simon said, and sat on the arm of her chair, 'and you must hope that you will have the wisdom to choose between the civilised and the barbarians. My dear cousin-by-marriage, you go too easily from one extreme to the other!'

'Well! Who suggested that I should go and have a look at the master race at work tonight? Who tensed up like a coiled spring when we met Gunther at the kafana that night?'

'Ah, that was when I recognised the barbarian, and when the likeness to his father made me ill. As for tonight, it was an experience for you, and you have not had many. Think of the people in this hotel – all twenty of them are German, and only the Einhardt woman is a savage. Frau Hersher is kind, a *good* woman, and with features as beautiful as her mind.'

'Yes,' Rowena admitted unwillingly. 'I admire her looks, and her manners, and the fact that she has such a good mind, and that she uses it. But she's no different from attractive people of other nations, is she? When you get a barbarous German, why are they so much more revolting than the dregs of any other race?'

Oliver laughed and pointed his pipe at Simon. 'She's got you there, my boy! I'll tell you what it is, Rowena. They were never civilised, never conquered by Rome. Even the English had about four hundred years of Roman rule, but the Germans had the Goths and the Vandals. In the old days when the Protestant Northerner and the Catholic Rhinelander and the Bavarian had a wonderful time fighting each other, they existed well enough within their own area, but once they were united, they had to find someone else to fight. They'll drop us right into it again if we're not careful! So, take individuals as you find them, but watch them as a nation.'

He grinned at her and went off to his tourist camp, and Rowena went upstairs with a headache, which didn't surprise her in the least. She took a couple of pills, but it was a long time before she got to sleep, and however much she willed herself to stop thinking, her mind was a whirling kaleidoscope of pictures and impressions and ideas. She didn't waken until ten o'clock, and then peered drowsily at her mother who had come in with a tray.

'Viktor insisted that you were to have a morning off,' Anne told her. 'He lectured Simon for badgering you, and me for allowing it, and threw a few insults at Oliver as well! He says you have a very good mind, that time will give you all the experience you need, and that we are to stop leading you in the way *we* think you should go!'

Rowena laughed as she used the sponge and towel Anne gave her. 'It *is* rather like being thrown in at the deep end! But I'm learning to swim, and wondering why I've done nothing but dog-paddle for twenty-one years!'

'H'm,' Anne said doubtfully. 'You're a born crusader, but you're apt to go for the things you can't change. If you were to put the same thought and energy into a cause like famine relief, you'd feel you'd achieved something.'

'You're thinking about when I go back home, aren't

128

you?' Rowena was thoughtful as she spread plum preserve on her toast, and then she shrugged. 'Everything will be so different then – the place, the people, what we talk about, every facet of daily life. I'll just have to wait and see how I settle in. Don't worry about me, darling. Keith will help me to keep my feet on the ground!'

'Yes – well, I'm glad you've got someone. By the way, the police have just been along to collect Gunther's car keys. His mother was almost having hysterics early this morning when they walked into the hotel. She was demanding a small saw, and because she refused to say what she wanted it for, the porter on duty was rather reluctant to go looking for one. The police had three, of different sizes, and they removed the box from Gunther's wrist, and then presented him with it. He didn't want it, but they made him take it, and neither he nor his mother will be welcome in this country ever again.'

'It's awful of me, but I can't feel the smallest bit sorry for either of them.'

'Neither can I,' Anne said. 'It turns my inside over when I think of all the wedding rings that were originally in that box. Oh – there was something else I came in to tell you. Viktor wants it made quite clear that you have a home here for the rest of your life if you want it. He means if – if you were to change your mind about getting married, or – or anything like that.'

Rowena laughed. 'Good heavens, I'm not likely to do that! You and he are the best advertisement for marriage I've ever seen, and I can hardly wait to go and do likewise! But it's dear of him to want me too, and I shall tell him he certainly won't have seen the last of me when I leave next month.'

Next month. The phrase seemed to hover on the air when she was alone again, and she looked round the room with a slight crease between her brows. It didn't seem possible that so different a person would be returning to London. She thought back to the years of school and college, to her former self-assurance, her enthusiasms, her gratitude for being born in a modern age when a woman could come to equal terms with men and with life. Men, women, politicians, diplomats of past generations had been so blind to true values, so unthinking, so careless of the welfare of those who were to follow after them. But the rising generation knew it all, they saw with clear, unclouded vision, they had come to rescue the tired, blasé, strife-torn old world, and if they were mocked for their pains, that was only what visionaries had to bear when they brought Truth to mankind.

Rowena laughed softly, wryly, and went over to the window. Maybe you knew you were grown-up when you could laugh over the high-flown attitudes you had struck in the past. Maybe each new generation would see themselves as the only rebels, martyrs, and visionaries who ever existed, forgetting that they had no exclusive rights to a spirit of youth which was as old as time. But the world must always have its youthful would-be reformers, and could never have got anywhere without them. They usually grew into responsible citizens who cared about their fellow-man whatever his creed, race, or colour. The danger came from the young reformers who saw little good outside their own particular cause, who refused to face the fact that human nature as a whole was very imperfect, and who believed that if everyone supported their cause, then everyone automatically became pure of motive and sinless in action.

And that, thought Rowena, is just about where I'd got to before I came out here.

She opened a drawer in the dressing-table, and looked at the heap of Keith's letters inside. He had written at length, at least once a week, affectionate and interesting

130

letters which had so successfully removed her feeling of guilt at staying where she was in spite of her promises. She was grateful to him for that, and happy to be going back to him, and they were both looking forward to living in the house they loved and appreciated, but oh, if there were only some way to have Keith, and the Pimlico house, and Yugoslavia too. But you couldn't expect to get everything you wanted from life. Nobody did. You had to make a choice and stay with it. Look at Mother and Viktor, loving each other so desperately for twenty-two years, and making yet a life for themselves and others, knowing they might never even meet again. As for Simon . . .

Rowena frowned and picked up her bath towel. Simon's affairs were none of her business, but it would be – well, interesting to know exactly what he did want from life. Natalya was pretty, even-tempered, affectionate, a good cook, but somehow she didn't measure up to the kind of woman Simon should have . . . she wasn't *enough* . . . there would be little communion of minds and spirits, because there were no deeps in Natalya's nature which could be called on.

Rowena decided that the making of sweeping statements and judgments was something she would have to curb, but later in the day she tried to draw Natalya out in conversation, and paid more attention to what was said than she had done before. It was disappointing to have to conclude that her judgment had been right, and that beauty covered a shallow if very pleasant nature. Possessions sparked off Natalya's interest, and she approved of Srebro Kara because it belonged to Viktor, rather than for the intrinsic beauty of the house itself. Many people loved houses and cars as status symbols, but many also appreciated them for their worth and beauty and utility. *Having* them was all that mattered to Natalya, who, for example, would never learn to drive, but who would want a car standing outside her house where it could be seen.

'She's had so little of her own,' Anne said, when Rowena mentioned the subject to her later. 'You'd be the same if you'd shared a small stone house in the mountains with six others in the family – especially if you were the youngest, and had to make do with hand-me-downs until you left home.'

'Oh, I understand that very well,' Rowena said quickly. 'I wouldn't dream of criticising anyone for wanting possessions of their own. But – you generally want them *for* something, a house for your husband and family, a car to make it easier to get around, clothes to make you feel good when you wear them, a boat for fishing and for pleasure. Natalya seems to want to – to gather these things in, and contemplate them all her life!'

Anne was thoughtful for a moment. 'I guess it's like the land-hunger you hear about. Few peasants would refuse more land if you gave it to them, even if they couldn't use it. But it would be *theirs*, something to show for their years on earth, something to pass on to their sons. Natalya is of that stock, dear, and none the worse for it. She'll make a very good wife in most of the ways that matter, and whatever her reasons for her ambitions, they'll probably be quite a help to her husband!'

'I suppose so,' Rowena murmured, and left it at that. Her own sense of disappointment must arise from her old habit of wanting perfection in an imperfect world. She wasn't going to get all she desired, and neither was Simon, and her heart jerked and then raced on as she realised that his loss mattered more to her than her own.

There were several wet, stormy days during the remaining weeks of her stay, when the tables had to be set up in the dining-room instead of in the vinery, and when Djordje looked sorrowful and patient in the garden until Marija

132

smuggled him in behind the reception desk, to a folded blanket in a corner. So, for Rowena, another illusion was exploded, that the Adriatic knew little but blue skies, blue water, and hot sunshine for most of the year.

But, like Uncle Oliver, she loved the faces of Dalmatia and Montenegro whatever guise they wore, and one misty day she went with him to meet some old friends in the small town of Žabljak near Crno Jezero, the Black Lake. Their way had been through massive beech trees and dense fir, along rocky defiles, and up twisting passes. Sometimes the curtain of mist parted to show strange shapes of the tumbled rocks and boulders – a girl with a water-jar on her head, a praying man, a soldier shouting defiance to the winds with both arms uplifted. And then they came to the lake, and the mist drifted away for good, and they watched the reflection of the huge mass of Mount Durmitor become clearer in the still waters.

They spent the afternoon at Žabljak, and before they drove out of sight, Oliver stopped by the roadside and looked back at the houses, the meadows, the woods, the foothills, and finally at the encircling peaks of the mountains.

'I must be out of my mind,' he said at last. 'This is where I belong. I spend most of the year in England, counting the weeks and the months until I can get back here. I brood, I drive Cousin Hilda mad, I can't settle in to the cosy life of a Gloucestershire village, and I've even outgrown trips to London. I'm a Scot, with a life spent in the British Army, so I do like everyone else and retire to somewhere in Britain. Why am I doing it?'

Rowena had to laugh at his sudden revelation, and then she sobered when she saw how serious he was. 'I – I suppose because it was the normal thing to do. Did you ever consider Australia or Canada or anywhere like that?'

'Not really. I hadn't any special friends there, and I

forgot that the ones I did have would be scattered all over the British Isles. But here – there are all the others, those I fought with, and admired, and loved,' – he shot her a glance from under bushy brows, daring her to comment, 'and who welcome me back like one of their own.'

'It's very, very strange,' Rowena said in a slow, thoughtful voice. 'First you with the Serbs in nineteen-sixteen, then your niece with Viktor in nineteen-forty-four or thereabouts, and now your grand-niece with – with no one in particular and everyone in general. What *is* it about this small country that catches and keeps us?'

'I'll tell you what I believe,' he said as he drove off again. 'Racial memories. Are you warm enough? We've a long way to go – should really have taken a couple of days for this trip, but neither of us wanted to afford the time now. Well, you remember your history, I suppose, the Armada and all that?'

She remembered the facts and the outcome, but little of the details, and her eyes widened as Oliver told of the thirty or more ships which had sailed from Ragusa, as Dubrovnik then was, to join the Grand Armada of Spain. He had thought vaguely that there had been twelve Illyrian ships, known as the Twelve Apostles, until he got interested in his own background, and went digging around in the public records and museums. The family surname of Stanwick had often made him curious, because it didn't seem to belong to any part of Argyll or Inverness. The Stanwicks had been around Morven for a very long time, but where had they come from?

His brother, Anne's father, recalled an old story of an uncle who had been interested in the same question, but he had never been able to trace beyond an eighteenth century Alexander Christopher Stanwick.

'That doesn't sound very Highland,' Rowena said. 'Did you get any further back?'

134

'No, but then my brother remembered that the uncle got very excited about the Tobermory Galleon, off the Island of Mull. It's still down there, but it's all silted over.'

'Yes, of course, wasn't she the *Florida* or the *Florencia* or something like that? It's strange that that part of Scotland has no tradition of knitting patterns like they have in the Shetlands. Aren't the Fair Isle patterns supposed to be Spanish or Moorish designs?'

Oliver grinned. 'So they say, but I refuse to believe it! They're Dalmatian designs if ever I saw one. Anyway, about fifty years ago, it was proved that that particular galleon couldn't have been the *Florida* which didn't exist on any Armada list, and it couldn't have been the *Florencia* because she was one of the lucky ones to get back to Spain. She was the ship named on the Spanish lists as the *San Juan de Sicilia, hailing from Ragusa*, and one of the Levantine squadron, and commanded by Don Diego Tellez Henriquez who was the son of the Commandant of Alcantara.'

'Well!' Rowena digested the information, her thoughts lingering with rising excitement on the phrase, *hailing from Ragusa*. 'Go on, what more did you find out?'

'The local clan chieftain was McLean of Duart who was a bit of a brigand, and for ever fighting with someone. In return for provisions, Henriquez hired out his men to McLean, and they seem to have had a whale of a time feuding all over Morven. But Walsingham's Secret Service got on to it, and a chap named John Smollett went to Tobermory, and the next thing was that the *San Juan de Sicilia* blew up, killing everyone on board, including Henriquez. The wreck sank to the bottom, where she still is, and I reckon Walsingham rubbed his hands and thought he was well rid of a bunch of trouble-makers.'

'But – where do the Stanwicks come in?'

'Ah, see what you think of this. One of the things they

have in this country is a marvellous system of maritime museums and records all over the place. Did you visit the Naval Museum and Library in Dubrovnik? You should. Fascinating. Anyway, when I knew which ship I was looking for, it was easy. One of the seamen who sailed from Ragusa on the *San Juan de Sicilia* was an Aleksandar Krstanović. The minute I saw it, I knew that Aleksandar hadn't been aboard when the ship was blown up. Somehow he managed to survive and become accepted in that countryside, and very likely it was a woman who made sure he did survive.'

'And he'd be proud of his name,' Rowena said slowly, 'and he'd want to keep it if possible. The nearest Anglicised name would be Stanwick, and the Krs bit would sound like Chris. So that's where the later Christopher came from. Oh, uncle Oliver, do you think that's really what happened?'

'I can't prove it to the hilt,' he said honestly, 'but it's enough for me. Nearly four hundred years ago, a man from this coast was cast ashore in the west of Scotland, and now, at last, he's coming home.'

'You've made up your mind then?' Rowena asked, and swallowed the lump in her throat, and blinked desperately to hide the tears.

Oliver sighed, and straightened his shoulders. 'Yes. Until now, it's seemed just a pleasant romantic mystery, but why leave it at that? Suddenly, I don't seem to have any choice. I'm coming back.'

'Have you told the story to Mother?'

'I've never told anyone. Maybe I didn't want to be argued out of my beliefs! But when you said you'd been caught and – and held by this country too, I had to give you what I believed to be the reasons. Your experience was too like my own. Anne's at home here too, but she had Viktor to draw her back. You and I just have the sense of belonging, without a particular person being involved.

136

It's funny – you're very like your father in looks, and I never felt you favoured our side of the family at all. But the Fairfax part of you must be only skin deep! I'm sorry – I really am – for visiting my impatience with the father on the daughter.'

'I'm sorry too,' Rowena said quietly, 'but you were perfectly justified in what you knew of us. My father saw himself as a crusader against spiritual evil, and I – well, the thought of another war made me a kind of crusader too. I'm still terrified of it, but not in the – the mindless way I was before, and I'm sorry I was always rude to you because you were a born fighting man and you were good at your job.'

He took his hand from the wheel for a second, and laid it over hers, and then they both lapsed into silence. This part of the road was rough, but the Land Rover took the bumps and the shale banks with ease, and Rowena sat watching the sun go down among the clouds in a blaze of scarlet and gold. She envied Oliver the decision which was suddenly so right for him, and knew a blank sense of loss because she had been looking forward more than she knew to seeing him in London and, as he had put it, keeping the language and the country green in their memories.

It was late when they got back to Srebro Kara, and as Rowena got stiffly out of the car, she saw Simon and Natalya returning from a stroll along the beach.

'Pity you and Simon didn't see each other first,' Oliver murmured. 'Then we'd all be coming home.'

Rowena laughed. 'Your romantic streak is working overtime! There's no point in marrying a man, and then spending the rest of life arguing. Mind you, I like him, and I think he likes me, but we'd never agree well enough to live together.'

Certainly Simon and Natalya got on very amicably, she

thought as they all went indoors together, and maybe they had a communion of spirit which she had never understood. It didn't have to show, as Anne's and Viktor's did, in the space of one revealing look.

All the guests were in, so Viktor shut the big door, and after coffee, Natalya and Marija went to bed. Oliver and Rowena dealt hungrily with the rice pilau and salad which had been kept for them, and Oliver told the others that he had decided to come back and settle in Žabljak. After the exclamations of surprise and pleasure, Anne looked at him thoughtfully.

'What will you *do*? It's very beautiful in the Mount Durmitor area, but doesn't it get snowed up in winter?'

'Not quite, and anyway it wouldn't matter. I'd be of independent means, as they call it, so I wouldn't be taking work from anyone else, but my friends there are a schoolmaster, a smallholder, a wood-carver, and a doctor. They've all got their own bits of land, and I'm sure they wouldn't mind some help. Then there's the hospital too – there might be several things a layman could do. I wonder if they've got a library? You know, like the trolley things that come round some of our wards about twice a week. Oh, I wouldn't be idle.'

Simon laughed. 'That I can easily believe! The only thing which surprises me is why you ever returned to England in the first place. It is natural, of course, for all people to "go home," but *you* have longed for this country as an exile would.'

So Oliver told them the story he had told Rowena, and found it accepted with no incredulity at all. The Armada, Viktor said, might have been Spanish in inception, but the crews were at least half Dalmatian, French, Italian, German, Irish, and even some Englishmen who had, with the others, a common nationality in the Church of Rome.

138

Simon smiled widely at Rowena. 'You see, Gospodjica Krstanović, you have come to your right place also! Could we not interest you in the position of chambermaid in this beautiful hotel?'

'I've had that job for three months,' Rowena said flippantly, 'but somehow I don't think it's my life's work! Anyway, although I love being here, that doesn't mean I've come to my right place. Mother has Viktor, Uncle Oliver has lots of old friends, but remember that where your treasure is, there shall your heart be also. My treasure is in London, so that seems to be the place for me.'

Her voice was light, and she was laughing at them, because she didn't dare join in an eager discussion of her heritage, her present, and her future. Their desire to keep her with them was like a tangible weight on her, and she knew that her own inclinations wouldn't let her judge the situation fairly. She had to get away from here, to look back with a judicious eye and a clear mind, to return to what she had always thought of as her future in her old and lovely home.

Viktor spread out his hands and looked at her with wry understanding. 'You are faithful, but you are also stubborn, and that is indeed a Slav characteristic. Part Scot, and part Slav – a most terrifying combination! Ah well, it is unjust of us to – how do you say it? – to gang up on you. We must all choose our own roads, and then we will have no one to praise or blame but ourselves if life does not turn out as we would wish. It is a sad subject, but your time to leave will soon be upon us. Have you thought of booking a flight? We must remember that travelling becomes very difficult during the high season.'

'I don't really want to fly,' Rowena said hesitantly. 'It's too quick, it doesn't give one time to – to adjust to the big difference between where one has been and where one is going. I'd like to leave here by boat, and sail along

139

the coast as far as Trieste. Then I could arrange about a train or a coach or a plane back to England. What about that steamer which calls in at Hercegnovi in the small hours?'

Viktor considered it. 'The journey takes two days, so you will need a cabin. It is not the most modern of the ships of that line, but it is comfortable enough and the service is good. We will go and see about it tomorrow.'

There were only tourist berths available, in a cabin for six, but Rowena didn't mind that. She was quite prepared to wrap herself in a rug and spend the night in a deckchair, as many travellers did in the summer. What mattered to her was that she would be alone, she would be able to give her emotions a rest after leaving Srebro Kara, and before meeting Keith again.

Viktor had already engaged two new girls for the rest of the season, so Rowena took life easier for her remaining days. She went swimming, she lazed on the beach with some of the hotel guests she liked, and she spent a lot of time with the donkeys in their field. They were very popular with guests who liked to ride off the beaten tracks, and they were also used for marketing, and by members of the family when the use of the jeep wasn't feasible. Rowena was sitting there one afternoon, in the shade of the trees along the back fence, when Anne came through the gate with a basket and stood laughing down at her daughter. There was cause enough for it, because Marija's little donkey, Petak, was lying with his head against Rowena's arm, Djordje was standing by her other shoulder and apparently whispering in her ear, and two more were grouped about her feet like heraldic symbols.

'Being a chambermaid may not be your life's work,' Anne said, 'but being a donkey-girl surely is! You'll have to get one to keep in the back garden in London!'

'They're such loving little beasts,' Rowena said with

a smile. 'They like people even more than dogs do, and their faces are quite beautiful. Did you come for one? Where are you going?'

'I'm taking a ham to Ivanka Nimani, and I'm going to talk to her about selling some of her lovely lace in the hotel. I've got a bottle of slivovica for Milos too, and I'm not in the mood for walking. As my adorable little Djordje isn't a beast of burden, which of your brood will you permit me to ride?'

'Any but Petak here,' Rowena said, scratching him behind the ears. 'Marija gave him to me – did you know? Not that I can really have him, but it was a sweet thought. Sit down for a few minutes. The new girls are managing fine.'

Anne sat down in the shade, and the donkeys eyed her with benevolence. More company! This *was* a splendid afternoon.

'About my wedding,' Rowena said slowly. 'I don't want you to think of coming to England for it. Victor won't be able to get away, and I know he'd be terrified of letting you out of his sight. You feel the same, and honestly, darling, I couldn't bear to part you both for a ceremony that will last about an hour at the most. Do believe me, it would make me very unhappy if you came, and if that sounds back-handed, it's meant in the nicest possible way!'

Anne sighed. 'I know that, and I love you for it, and even if it's selfish of me, I have to agree with you. You know, a few months ago I would have been quite ready to believe you wouldn't mind whether your mother was hovering over the bride or not! Now we both want it, and can't have it, which is rather sad.'

'No,' Rowena said quietly. 'It's been worth it, and we've both learned a thing or two since then. Uncle Oliver will have to return to England to settle his affairs, and maybe I can fix dates so that he'll be able to give me away. He and

Keith will just have to bear with each other for that one day!'

Anne made a face as she rose to go to the small stable for a saddle blanket. 'Oil and water, my dear! I wish – oh well, never mind. Will you still be here when I come back?'

'I don't think so. I must start my packing – isn't it amazing that the things I brought for a fortnight have been more than enough to last me for three months! When I – when I come again, I'll have a better idea of what to bring for you and the duchess. She does love perfumed soaps and shampoos and powders.'

'Just bring yourself,' Anne said, and led her donkey away.

Rowena sat watching the former Mrs. James Fairfax, sandalled and bare-legged, guiding her mount through the gate as if she had never known any other form of transport. And here was Miss Fairfax, who had always known where she was going, who had never had time for profitless dreams, and who had had life tamed and brought to heel – here she was, dreaming in a meadow with a bunch of donkeys, quite happily forgetting the troubled world she had been so desperate to save from its own folly. From correct Belgravia to the unpredictable Balkans in several difficult lessons. It was really too amusing for words – only, one didn't somehow feel like laughter.

9

THE coastal steamer called at Hercegnovi in the early hours of the morning, and it was still dark when Rowena took a last glance round her room in case she had forgotten anything. Her door was open, and when Simon came for her luggage, he looked at the ikon of the Angel of Mileševo.

'You are not taking it?' he asked. 'Viktor was sure you would like to have it for your own.'

'She wouldn't belong in London,' Rowena said slowly. 'Let her stay here, above the bed, for the delight of the next "family guest" who sleeps in this room. I'd rather remember her where she is, and anyway, it would be like robbing a church to take her away!'

They went down to breakfast, and found Natalya as wide awake and cheerful as if her working day always began before dawn. Viktor and Anne were keeping up the façade of lightheartedness too, and only Marija showed a woebegone face to match her spirits.

In the mixture of Serbo-Croatian, German, and English in which they usually conversed, Marija told Rowena not to forget her own tiny stone house in the mountains near Izvor.

'It is empty while I am here,' she explained, 'but a good neighbour keeps it clean and sweet for me. If you should ever need to be alone – and it is good for us all to be alone sometimes – you would like my little house. You love mountains, and they are so beautiful there. And you must not forget Petak, because if you set him on the road from here, he would take you straight home.'

'Thank you, duchess,' Rowena said gratefully. 'It's lovely to know that I can go there if I want to. And bless you for giving me Petak – I'll have to come back even if it's just to see him!'

The meal went on to the accompaniment of laughter and conversation, and Rowena felt that if she didn't get outside for a while she would either collapse or be sick. With a murmured excuse of seeing whether Djordje and Petak were awake, she went out through the garden door and leaned weakly against the wall. Almost at once, Simon was there, supporting her across one arm while his cool hand curved round her brow.

'Slow, deep breaths,' he said quietly. 'There is plenty of time. It was too warm in there.'

She did as he suggested, and after a while her surroundings steadied, and a relieving coolness made her shiver a little. Simon took his hand from her brow, and she leaned back against him and looked along the lightening garden.

'It wasn't the heat,' she admitted. 'Do you know that saying – "to go away is to die a little"? No matter how much one has to look forward to, to leave a place where one has been very happy is like a small death.'

'There is another half to that saying,' Simon told her, 'and I am not fond of it. It is that "to return is to know what it is to be a ghost." Oh, Rowena, little cousin, I wish I had the right to ask you not to go away!'

She stood very still within his encircling arm, dwelling with startled disbelief on the pain and longing in his voice. Before she could say anything, there came the sound of a footstep on the threshold, and she and Simon were standing apart when Natalya joined them.

'It is useless to wait for those lazy animals,' Natalya

said almost apologetically. 'They will not appear for you, and – and Viktor has gone for the car, because the steamer does not wait for long at the pier. It is a pity that Uncle Oliver has not returned from Nis, but he will be in London for your wedding, will he not?'

'I – yes, he's promised to give me away,' Rowena managed. 'He'll be able to tell you all about it when he comes to live in Žabljak. And he can bring the photographs and the – wedding the cake. I must get going.'

She turned abruptly and went indoors, glad that her mother and Marija were already out in the hall, and that there was no one to witness the sudden panic that must be plainly written on her face. The small death of parting was showing more vividly than she had expected or believed possible.

Simon went on to the car, and Natalya halted by the reception desk and turned a long look on Rowena. 'Keith loves you dearly,' she said with cool emphasis, 'just as I love Simon. You have so much, and it would be cruel to add what does not belong to you. Do you understand me?'

Rowena stared at her, feeling the blood drain from her face. 'I wouldn't dream of taking what was yours! I – there's never been any suggestion – how can you even *think* that I – that Simon had any such thing in mind!'

'I ask your pardon if I have wronged you,' Natalya said calmly, but her eyes showed that she believed otherwise. 'It is not easy for people like us to feel secure. Too often we have been left with nothing, and one becomes afraid that there is no longer justice left in the world.'

'You have nothing to fear from me,' Rowena vowed. 'Good-bye.'

She walked quickly away, and at the door Marija gave her a small package. 'It is the New Testament in our Serbian language. It was my husband's. I – it is not much.

145

but it will remind you of our lessons together, and it is a good book to read and to have for a companion.'

Rowena couldn't say anything, but she and Marija had no need of words. Viktor touched the horn gently, and Rowena ran out to join Simon in the back of the jeep. Everything had been said, and it was a quiet foursome which strolled on to the pier some time later. The steamer had just come in, several passengers were going aboard, and when Viktor saw the man who was checking tickets, he smiled with satisfaction.

'It is Ivan Mitrev,' he told Rowena, 'and we have been friends all our lives. He will look after you – he is in charge of the tourist class, and he rules with a rod of iron!'

Ivan stood under a lamp, a tall, broad man with a grey crew cut, and when he looked up and saw Viktor, his eyes widened and then almost disappeared in crinkles of laughter. His long arms and big hands were outstretched as he came forward, and after he had greeted his old friend, he looked down at Anne with pleasure.

'You have done well,' he told Viktor, 'but if she had seen me first, you would not have had a chance! And to think that she brought you a daughter also!' He smiled at Rowena, and patted her shoulder. 'You will enjoy the journey to Trieste, and you will be as comfortable as I can arrange. There are already two ladies in the cabin – do you wish to sleep until breakfast time?'

'I'd like to have a chair on deck and watch the sun come up,' Rowena said, and Ivan nodded.

'Of course. Viktor, you may all come aboard for a few minutes – no longer! Find a deck chair and put it in shelter – the wind is from the east today. When we have sailed, I will bring a rug, but there are more passengers and I must stay here.'

Viktor, who was used to the Adriatic steamers, found the sheltered spot he wanted, and when he had arranged

146

the deck chair, he looked down at Rowena and touched her cheek. 'Whatever you do,' he said softly, 'we shall always be close in spirit. I believe – and do you not believe it also? – that Oliver's "romance" about the seaman Krstanovic is the only possible truth. I have no doubt that he was happy in the home he made on Morven, but there must have been times when he thought of Illyria with great longing.'

'As I shall,' Rowena murmured, and when he had kissed her and walked quickly away, she looked after him with wistful eyes. She thought that Simon would have been the next to follow him, but Anne got in first with a brief, warm farewell, and when she had gone, Simon lifted Rowena's hand to his lips. She trembled, recalling Natalya's accusing eyes, knowing that the other girl had had a right to speak as she had done.

'No more time,' Simon said, 'no more words. This is at last the day in which I refused to believe! Now that it is upon us, do you think we could be "kissing cousins"? It is a charming American phrase, is it not?'

'Yes,' Rowena agreed unsteadily, and she clung to him as he placed both arms around her and kissed her with a passionate and despairing tenderness. Her response was immediate, and her senses seemed to drift into a region of dark delight where nothing mattered but the touch of this man's lips, and where Keith and Natalya and everyone else were utterly forgotten. When Simon at last lifted his head and looked down at her, memory returned with chill dismay, and she made to draw back.

'I know,' Simon said, and kissed her again. 'We are not free, but we are not perfect either. One must have something to keep – something to remember – a lighted window to show the way on a long, dark night.'

He let her go, slowly, and then framed her face in his hands and claimed her lips once more. No memories of

147

other people, no bustle of departure from the quayside could prevent her responding generously and gladly to this last kiss. She was going to have need of a lighted window in the darkness too.

Almost before she realised it, Simon was gone, and the ship was drawing away from the pier. The sky was light now, and soon the sun would pour its golden warmth over the dark mountains of Montenegro. The three from Srebro Kara stood with arms linked until Rowena could see them no more, and as the breeze freshened out to sea she turned up her collar and dropped to her chair. She had a fleeting thought that she ought to be much more upset over her departure, and the onset of a few tears wouldn't have surprised her. But her eyes were wide and tearless, and her emotions were curiously frozen, as if they had gone into cold storage during this transition from a random summer to a predetermined future.

Ivan brought her a rug, but he merely smiled and said nothing as he wrapped it round her and returned to his duties. Rowena's last Adriatic sunrise was a dramatic one, all gold and crimson among wind-puffed clouds on a cool green sky. It was the first time she had seen Dubrovnik from the sea, so beautiful in the golden light of morning, so unforgettable in its poetry of towers and red roofs and spires and ancient fortresses. But too soon, the old town was out of sight, and crowds of passengers poured on to the steamer at Gruz harbour. And so it was, all through the day, and Rowena was glad of her sheltered corner which she left only for meals in the crowded tourist saloon. She was interested in the groups of boys who came aboard at almost every port, boys of about sixteen who carried small kit-bags and who were seen off by what looked like the entire population of their towns. There were songs too, and those left behind on the piers swayed to their own music while the boys on the steamer waved and laughed, and some of them wept a little and tried not to show it.

Rowena discovered that they were all going to Pula to join the Navy, and when Ivan wished to seat her with three other women in a quieter corner for dinner, she laughed in answer to the grinning invitation from some of the boys at the long table. Ivan stood and scowled at them while they placed Rowena with much ceremony at the head of the table, and then he smiled and shrugged when one of them assured him that they would look after his 'English treasure'.

Only a few of the boys spoke English, and conversation was in the usual mixture of German and Italian and Serbo-Croatian, and because several belonged to seafaring families, Rowena told them the story of Aleksandar Krstanović. They loved the romance of the Illyrian seaman wrecked on the shores of Morven, but she was amused by their disapproval of his mission. The Spanish Armada, they said, was a wicked enterprise, poorly carried out, and if this Krstanović was her ancestor, it was to be hoped that he had learned some sense during his lifetime in Scotland.

'Ah,' said Rowena, 'he came as an enemy, but he stayed as a friend. That was sense, wasn't it?'

'Out!' Ivan ordered, shooing them like a sheep-dog. 'Look at the queue waiting to come in! Miss Fairfax, it will be warm down in your cabin. Do not permit these ruffians to keep you talking on deck in this cold wind.'

But Rowena was loth to let go of companions who had such alert and questing minds, and they all sat huddled against a bulkhead out of the wind, to argue and discuss and even to learn something new. One of the younger boys, slight and fair, fell asleep against Rowena's shoulder, and before long he had drooped to her lap while the boy on his other side slept against his back. Someone put out a hand to waken them, but Rowena stopped them. The sleeper in

149

her lap was one who had wept when he left his family behind, and the warm weight of him was somehow the embodiment of his nation, her own people, whom she loved and was leaving. Most of the group were dozing, and she sat on, thinking and remembering, when she looked up and saw Ivan watching her with outraged eyes. She put a finger to her lips, eased her way out of the sleeping bodies, and followed Ivan to his pantry.

'Drink,' he ordered, handing her a cup of steaming coffee. 'Viktor will have my head if he finds out that I permitted you to play nursemaid to these brats!'

Rowena smiled. 'I won't tell him, but he would understand anyway. They were so friendly, and they've just left home for the first time. Poor lambs, I hope your Navy will be kind to them.'

'Kind!' Ivan snorted. 'It will be the best thing in the world for them!' He looked at her for a moment, and his eyes held warmth. 'I did not have much time to talk with Viktor, but you are going back to Srebro Kara, are you not?'

'I'm returning to England to get married,' she said abruptly, 'but it's quite possible that I'll be back for holidays from time to time. I – I'll have to wait and see how things work out.'

Ivan started to speak and then changed his mind, and Rowena was grateful because she had no wish to invite further pressures to keep her where she was. She had to get right away from all the tough, entwining cords which were binding her to this country before she could look back and consider their strength.

She slept through the night although she would have liked to have seen the young sailors get off at Pula, and an Englishwoman told her at breakfast that they had made plenty noise about it.

'Funny lot, the Yugoslavs,' the woman concluded.

'I was quite thrilled to be coming by myself to a Communist country, but it's no different from anywhere else. Except that they're not very well off, and they're a bit backward compared with us. Funny how they let you go where you like without asking questions – I'd never have believed that Communists were so easy-going.'

'They're not on the whole,' Rowena said thoughtfully. 'I've been here for three months, and I would say the average person is a human being first, a Yugoslav second, and a Communist third. And even then, they're not all party members. They can talk to anyone they like, read what they like, and as far as I can see, there's no censorship such as you find among dedicated Communists like the Russians. No, the Iron Curtain doesn't start here, and I wouldn't look on this as typical Communism at all.'

The conversation drifted to other subjects, and Rowena smiled to herself as she remembered that a few months before, she wouldn't have known the difference between one shade of political belief and another. All her scorn had been reserved for the 'decadence' of the western democracies, and she had lent too willing an ear to the parrot cries for peace at any price. She had begun to realise that some prices could be too monstrous to pay.

When the steamer docked at the end of the run, Rowena took her time about going ashore. Trieste was Italian soil, and when she stepped off the gangway she would be severing the last of her summer's bond with Yugoslavia. Ivan came to her where she hesitated on the deck, and he looked at her suitcases.

'You have everything?' he asked. 'Come, we will find a taxi. Are you going to the airport?'

She decided that she might as well go there as anywhere else. She had made no arrangements, because a slow journey home had seemed a necessary interval for thought, but now she knew that she could settle nothing before she reached London. She was really tired for the first time in months, her thoughts were incoherent anyway, and it was suddenly a good idea to be alone. So Ivan said 'Dovid-jenja' as if he knew she would like to hear it for the last time instead of 'Good-bye,' shut the taxi door, and walked slowly and thoughtfully back on board the steamer.

Rowena had to wait for a flight to Rome, and then she had to wait there for another one to London, and she finally got through the Customs in the early hours of the next morning. By the time she reached her own door, she was dazed with fatigue, and when the cab driver put her cases in the hall, she closed the door after him and stood leaning against it with her eyes shut. She roused herself enough to scribble a note for Mrs. Waring who would come in during the day as usual, and knowing that her bed would be made up and aired, she went wearily upstairs.

When Mrs. Waring brought tea and toast at four in the afternoon, Rowena stared blankly for a moment and then smiled and stretched. 'I'd forgotten where I was. After two very uncomfortable nights, this bed is sheer heaven! Bless you, Mrs. Waring, I hope I haven't made you stay late.'

'Oh, indeed no. I've been in every day since you left, and I must say it's nice to have someone wanting a cup of tea again! My, but you're a lovely colour. I've always wanted to go a sort of golden tan like that, but I just manage to stay plump and pink! Are you rested after your sleep?'

'I should be,' Rowena said doubtfully, as she poured out a cup of tea, 'but I must admit I don't feel too bright. I've been rising early and going to bed late and – truly! – working very hard most days. We wrote you about the wedding, but Mother has sent you a heap of photographs, and a lace cloth, and I've a few other things for you as well.'

Mrs. Waring beamed. 'Oh, lovely! Your mother sounded very happy when she wrote, and I'm dying to see the photographs. I'll go and run a bath for you, and you'll feel the better of it.' She paused in the doorway and looked back. 'Mr. Manning rang up last night to ask when you were coming home. He was a bit anxious about it, because he has to go to some television conference in the west country in a few days. If he should ring again while you're in the bath—'

'Ask him to come round this evening, please. I didn't know myself when I would arrive, and I was too exhausted to start sending telegrams from London Airport. Is there much in the larder?'

'I stocked up after I read your note today, so you'll be all right for a good meal tonight. Ah, Mr. Manning came round several times when I was here on a Saturday.'

'He did?' Rowena's eyebrows rose. 'He never mentioned it in any of his letters. What did he want?'

Mrs. Waring shrugged lightly. 'Just to see that everything was all right, I suppose. I made him some tea, and he just wandered round the house for a while. It *is* a nice place, you know, and I think he came because he liked it.'

'Yes, he does,' Rowena agreed, and smiled a little. 'I'm sure I can't think why it should remind me of Henry the Fifth trying on his father's crown before the old man was dead! Oh well, no doubt he'll mention it when he comes round tonight.'

When Keith arrived about eight o'clock, Rowena had dinner in the oven, and had changed into a dress of white, clinging jersey. She had washed her hair that afternoon, deciding that she rather liked the sun-bleached streak which waved back among the shining, pale brown strands.

'Darling, you look quite gorgeous,' Keith said after he had kissed her into breathless, almost-embarrassed protest. 'I've never seen you with a real tan before, and it makes

153

your grey eyes go all shining and silver! Oh, *how* I've missed you! I was reduced to haunting this house on Saturdays, just so that I could catch a drift of your perfume from that bowl on your dressing-table!'

'Oh, my dear, you didn't!' Rowena said with sudden humility, hating herself for her previous thought that he had come because he liked to picture living in the house. 'Your letters were so – so sweet and generous, but you never once let me know that you'd got to the stage of chasing my perfume!'

Keith laughed lightly as he followed her into the kitchen. 'Oh well, I didn't want to spoil things for you by letting you know I was pining! But here you are, and I can hardly believe it, and please, when can we get married?'

The fork Rowena was holding clattered to the floor, and her voice sounded nervous in her own ears. 'We – we'll have to wait till Uncle Oliver gets back to England. He's the only family I've got left, and he must be here. Did I tell you he was going back to Yugoslavia for good?'

'M'm, and a good idea too. He'll suit them, and they'll suit him, and they can all have a lovely time fighting their battles all over again. But I promise I won't say anything like that if he agrees to grace our wedding!'

Rowena didn't pursue the subject of Uncle Oliver. She was too tired to argue about it, and she knew that Keith would never understand her change of heart regarding the old man. She didn't tell him about Aleksandar Krstanović either, but she did tell him about Gunther Kleist and his midnight digging for his 'legacy'.

'He couldn't have known what was in the box,' Keith said after a few moments. 'It's the same old tale of buried treasure the world over – people just have to go digging for it when they get a clue, whether it's in their own country or not.'

'Gunther knew,' Rowena said tiredly, 'and so did his

mother who was waiting for him at their hotel. He was in tears of fury because all that was left for him was a few gold teeth.'

They were in the drawing-room, side by side on the couch, and Keith frowned unhappily as he looked at the summer arrangement of foliage on the hearth. 'I find that hard to believe. I liked Gunther, and I'm sure he was just being curious about the "X marks the spot" story, as most of us would be. I suppose he was lucky your friends didn't shoot him there and then!'

'How very odd,' Rowena said after a thoughtful pause. 'You are so thoroughly taking the part of the evil-doer against those who were wronged, that you've forgotten all about ordinary human justice. Actually, Viktor and Simon never laid a finger on him – *I* was the one who wanted to tear him apart! And that wouldn't have been justice either, because he was merely a sewer-rat who tried to profit from his father's scavenging.'

Keith gave her a sober look, and took her hand in his. 'You've changed a lot, my sweet. Even your voice has a kind of belligerence. Are we going to argue the toss every time there's a mention of Yugoslavs or Germans or justice?'

'I don't see why not, if we both feel strongly enough. If I have changed, it's because academic questions became face-to-face problems for the first time in my life. I recall your telling me that one of the things you loved about me was that I was intellectually honest. I hope I still am, but will you only approve of my conclusions if they're the same as your own?'

'Oh, darling, no, of course not! It's just that we were always so very much at one in our thoughts and our views, and now we seem to have moved apart. We'll have to negotiate a cease-fire line! I've remembered something too. You often used to say how inspiring it was to belong to our branch of the peace society, so many of us with a common purpose, all belonging to a young movement that was really going somewhere.'

'Any movement, going in any direction,' Rowena said reflectively. 'I gave *so* much to it, I almost ran myself into the ground trying to forward the cause of peace. I joined our society because its ideals seemed to be the nearest to my own, and how marvellous it felt to be in with a crowd who all thought as I did! My little ego had a splendid time for more than four years, but oh heavens, wasn't I a useless member of the human race!'

She leaned forward and poured more coffee for them both, aware of Keith's simmering irritation, and wishing he would take her up on what she had said. This restraint was anything but natural, and she was certain they were both hiding what they really felt and what they really thought. She was tired and confused and argumentative, but the memory of Keith's forbearance when he had left her behind at Srebro Kara, the vivid phrasing of his pleasant letters, and his kindly concern for her welfare all added up to a chain which was binding her to a future she couldn't bear to contemplate. How true it was that by letting go of those you loved, you bound them to you more closely than ever! Keith *must* be aware that they weren't the same people who had parted three months before, that there was a gulf between them which nothing could bridge. And yet, he was – well, gritting his teeth and holding on, as if the words that might clear the air would also finish whatever it was that remained of their old association.

'You're tired out, darling,' Keith said at last, 'so I'll take myself off. I'm due at this conference the day after tomorrow, so I won't see you before I go. I've been trying to get out of taking over from one of our chaps in Plymouth for three weeks, but – maybe it would be just as well if I stayed down there. You need time to settle down to being back in London. Will you call and see Mother? I know she's looking forward to seeing you.'

'Yes, I'll be glad to go and see her,' Rowena said, and sighed faintly. 'I'm sorry I've been such poor company tonight. The truth is, I'm homesick for a place you can't stand, and that makes me slightly blue!'

Keith nodded. 'I could guess that. Don't worry, we can come to terms about that, as well as about everything else!' He went out to the hall, and smiled down at her as he put his hand on the door-knob. 'Tell Uncle Oliver to come back as soon as possible!' He kissed her warmly, opened the door, and went away.

Rowena shot the bolts, and then pressed her hands to her temples and stood still, alone as she had never been before, and aghast at her reactions to the embrace of the man she was still supposed to marry. She hadn't met him after long absence with the joyous abandon of a woman in love, and for a short time she had put that down to physical weariness. But tiredness had nothing to do with the outrage she had felt in the last five minutes, with the cold astonishment that anyone should *dare* to hold her and kiss her like that when she belonged to Simon . . . ah, dear heaven, Simon . . . 'we are not free,' he had said, but they had clung to each other with a desperate and irresistible devotion . . . 'leave me what belongs to me,' Natalya had pleaded, and she had promised Natalya that she had nothing to fear . . . not realising even then that loving Simon must take all she had to give, so that there was nothing left for Keith or for any other man . . . she had tried so hard to keep the farewell incident in 'its place,' she had refused to daydream about it, she was going to come home and lay out all her plans and her hopes and her emotions for a rigid mental inspection . . . and she had forgotten the heart that will flower unbidden, and which will take no notice of what is best, or of what ought to be, or even of what is right . . .

She opened the bottle of slivovica she had brought home, and as soon as she smelt its dry, evocative fragrance she was back in Srebro Kara, and she closed her eyes to hold on to the moment and to pretend that by some miracle she was really there. But Natalya was there too, and with a wry curve to her mouth, Rowena poured herself a drink, put out the lights, and went upstairs. Natalya and Keith . . . two innocent interlopers who deserved better than the hostility she felt for them then.

She spent the next morning shopping, and while she had lunch, she watched the people around her with faint envy. They all had something to do, something to keep them occupied and interested, but she had had no intention of looking for a job when she came home. There was going to be plenty to do in getting the house ready for Mr. and Mrs. Keith Manning; a wedding, however modest, needed preparation; and there was to be ample time after marriage to decide whether she wanted to return to the interior decorating business or not.

But the house was already as she had always wanted it to be. Even if she were still to marry Keith, no wedding date could be fixed until Uncle Oliver returned from Yugoslavia. And her last contacts with her career had been over three months ago, a remote, unreal period now that so much had happened in between.

She left her half-finished meal, paid the bill, and went out, impatient with the lethargy that had attacked her body and her mind so that it was too much trouble to plan anything, and too impossibly exhausting to carry out any plans that might get made. She had had lunch out only to save herself bother, intending to go home immediately afterwards, but she found herself walking up Regent Street until she came to the Yugoslav National Tourist

Office. The photographs in the window were large, coloured, and almost three-dimensional, and she gazed at one of Kotor as if she had been a starving child outside a baker's. The view was the one she and Simon had seen at dawn from the top of Mount Lovčen, but it was just a picture, and instead of a loved voice and a chorus of bird-song, she heard only the roar of traffic and snatches of conversation from passers-by.

She turned away abruptly, and took a taxi home, and when she got indoors, Mrs. Waring looked at her with concern.

'You're not looking at all up to the mark, dear. Maybe you've been doing too much. You go in and sit down, and I'll bring you a nice cup of tea in five minutes.'

When the tea arrived, Rowena was sitting back on the couch with her eyes closed, and after a moment she looked up. 'What am I going to *do*, Mrs. Waring? I'm so homesick for Yugoslavia that I could howl like a lost pup! As for Keith – absence hasn't made the heart grow fonder, but I don't trust my own feelings any more. How can I be sure I won't change back again in a month?'

'You can't,' Mrs. Waring said thoughtfully as she sat down. 'You just have to go along with the situation until you haven't any doubts left one way or the other. Marriage – to most of us anyway – isn't something you can walk away from if it doesn't turn out to be quite what you expected, and we all feel we can't afford to make a mistake.'

She smiled and twisted her wedding ring. 'I got in a terrible panic about a week before my wedding, and I shocked my Charles by saying that marriage seemed as permanent as death! To be honest, I didn't lose my doubts until I'd been married a few days, but I haven't had a single one since.'

'Mother never had any at all,' Rowena said. 'She was so sure, and so much in love with Viktor from the beginning, and maybe that's what's influencing me. Oh well, I'll take your advice and weather the depression for the time being!'

'Have you prayed about it? Oh, I know that's no more fashionable than looking on marriage as a lifelong bond, but it's helped me often when I didn't know which way to turn. It's only in the last few years that I've found out what a blessing it is to have faith in the workings of the Almighty and I often wish I'd had it when I was younger.'

'Prayer?' Rowena echoed, and remembered the surprise in Simon's voice when they had been at Kotor and he had asked her: 'Do you not believe that there is a God?' She remembered Marija's gift of the New Testament, and the fact that Viktor and Simon and so many others had gone to church to give thanks when they heard about the gifts pouring into earthquake-stricken Skopje. She had never realised how many of the people she deeply respected possessed what a famous writer had once called 'an invisible means of support.'

'You think about it,' Mrs. Waring advised her as she went out with the tray, and Rowena did just that. She didn't get very far, because the years of indifference had bred only a delight in the King James version of the Scriptures, without understanding of the message or the meaning of the beautiful words. But they were certainly worth another look, and with a stirring of interest she hadn't known for days, Rowena went to change before visiting Keith's mother.

Mrs. Manning seemed very pleased to see her again, admitting that her son was only just fit to live with when his fiancée was away from him for three months. Rowena had brought all her Yugoslav photographs, and although Mrs. Manning was interested in those which showed Keith or Rowena, the scenic ones evoked merely: 'So wild and rough, dear, and those mountains are quite gloomy, don't you think? Did Keith tell you I went to Eastbourne for a week? Such very pretty countryside around there. And these are the wedding pictures – why, the bridegroom is quite *old*, isn't he? Somehow I never thought of your mother marrying a man with *white* hair.'

'Oh, it's thick and curly and beautiful,' Rowena said cheerfully, 'and at forty-three he's only three years older than Mother. The minute I saw him, I knew why she'd never been able to forget him, and they're terribly happy together.'

'That's nice dear,' Mrs. Manning said with a vague, uncomprehending look at the bride and groom who were smiling at each other in a trance of contentment. Mrs. Manning's vocation as A Mother had been all-embracing, and Rowena knew a sudden surge of compassion for the husband who had died when Keith was sixteen.

Mrs. Manning sighed and glanced at the clock. 'Such a pity Keith had to go down to Plymouth, but I hope he'll get out of staying there for more than a week. He's been like a cat on hot bricks all summer, dear, just because you were away for so long. I hoped – well, I thought he would come home last night and tell me the date of the wedding was all fixed. Have you no idea at all when your great-uncle will be coming back to England?'

'No, I'm just waiting to hear from him. I – he shouldn't be too long now.'

She gazed unseeingly at the photographs in her lap, frowning a little. So Keith had only told his mother the bare facts, and had said nothing about the uncomfortable evening they had spent together. She felt a pang of guilt because she was using Uncle Oliver as a pretext for her own cowardice and irresolution. She had hailed Keith's business trip with relief, because it meant more time to think, more time to 'settle down' as he had called it, but surely it was only postponing the inevitable parting?

And yet – they had cared enough once to become engaged. They had eagerly looked forward to sharing their lives, they had laughingly chosen the names for their children, and they had even planned the elegant parties they would give in the Georgian house. Where had it all gone, that uncomplicated delight in living?

Her panic of the night before had faded in the memory of Keith's patience and loving-kindness. If he wanted her so much, wasn't it better to bring happiness to a man who loved her, than to cry for the unattainable moon throughout a lonely and a selfish life? Maybe the memory of Simon would fade one day too, so that it would no longer seem wrong that any other man should hold her in his arms.

10

KEITH returned from the West Country after two weeks, and Rowena found that she had 'settled down' to a greater extent than had seemed possible on the day she arrived home. She was quite sure now that she had fallen out of love with Keith, but her own heart ached so much for Simon that she shrank from inflicting the same pain on Keith. She knew it was spineless and stupid not to care much about her own future now that she couldn't have what she wanted, but surely it would be some compensation to know that she would be giving Keith the future he wanted.

She shrugged away from the thought that a compensation was something that never quite compensated, and took up her life in London almost where she had left it. She dined out with Keith and went to the cinema or the theatre, and instead of going out to work she cleaned the house from the attics down. The only thing she didn't do was attend the meetings of the peace society, and Keith accepted the fact that she was still thinking out her attitude to the movement.

She wrote many more letters than she had ever done, and she pounced on those from Srebro Kara with a trembling eagerness that told her she was a long way from the day when memory would start to fade. She took time off now and then to go to the zoo, always ending up with the donkeys, wondering when she would see Petak again, and picturing Djordje tapping into the hall on his delicate little hooves as he went to the blanket Marija kept for him behind the reception desk. She called such days her escapes to 'wallowing in nostalgia,' and although she laughed at herself for foolish indulgence, she clung with frightening persistence to every evocation of her time in Yugoslavia.

One day she went to the Tower of London just because Simon had mentioned it when he spoke of tourists crowding the historical and lovely places of the world. She bought a post-card there, knowing that Simon would remember, and she was just about to write a conventional greeting when she thought of the inscription on the old carving in the square at Kotor. So, with a faint smile, she wrote: '*Pax tibi, Simon, amicus meus.*'

Some time later she had a card from Natalya and a letter from Anne. Natalya's words were cryptic – 'Now we have the house, so that is a beginning. I hope your plans go well also, and that we have good news from you soon.'

Rowena frowned and then opened her mother's letter. The first item of news was that Uncle Oliver was held up in Žabljak where he was making arrangements for his permanent home, and although he would try to be back in England in about a month, he couldn't make any promises. The next item was that Milos Nimani was dead, that his sister Ivanka was going to work and live at Srebro Kara, and that Simon was taking over the small stone house where Milos had waited so long and so patiently for Colonel Kleist.

'Natalya won't like *that*,' Rowena said aloud, recalling the other girl's naive delight in the size and importance of Srebro Kara. The Nimani house had only four rooms including the kitchen, and although there was space for the addition of a bathroom, that didn't mean that Simon would be able to have one installed as soon as he moved in.

Rowena looked again at the post card, and realised that the house was exactly what Natalya said it was – a beginning. If a girl had Simon, she needn't care where she lived as long as he was around somewhere. And a girl like Natalya would never forget that Srebro Kara itself beckoned in the future, and that Simon was the only male heir.

Oh, it wasn't *good* enough! Rowena walked up and down, her heels making angry whorls in the pile of the carpet, her arms crossed as if she were cold.

Simon shouldn't be merely a passport to someone else's advancement in life . . . he was so worthy of being loved for himself alone . . . he should have the best there was . . .

'Myself, in fact,' Rowena murmured, and with a mirthless laugh she sat down and faced the truth that that wasn't necessarily so. Even Anne had said that Natalya would be a good wife in all the ways that mattered. Simon was never cut out to be a monk, and a farewell kiss and some fervent whispered words weren't enough on which to build a revolt that would change the lives of four people. If he had wanted her badly enough, he would never have let her go.

Meanwhile, she was depending on Uncle Oliver to keep her from making a final decision about marrying Keith, and the awful thing was that Keith knew it and was trying to pretend that nothing had changed. For a man of his forthright temperament, it must have been like walking on eggs, and Rowena was a little awed by the outward discipline of his emotions.

She finally decided to attend one of the peace society meetings. She had been so involved in all the activities of the movement for years, that she had found nothing of the same absorbing interest to take their place, and whatever the imperfections of the society, its great aim of peace between nations was well worth working for.

Their branch had a new Chairman, a vicar from the

West End, and after seeing him on television, Rowena was looking forward to meeting him. At least he was articulate, and he had no time for slogans and timeworn phrases about the nuclear age.

The meeting was on a Saturday afternoon, and after lunch, Keith and Rowena walked along Cornhill to the hall. 'I rang you last night,' Keith said, 'but I didn't let it go on too long in case you were in the bath!'

'I was in church, and I got home after ten.'

'Church! On a Friday night?'

Rowena laughed. 'Why not? It's a Bible study series, and I went to the first one out of curiosity. I've been going ever since because it's interesting and very well done. Like to come? The series is about St. Paul's relevance to the present day.'

'Um, I never did care much for Paul's views on life. He was so much *against* everything that might please a mere mortal.'

'That's just what he wasn't, which is why the course is so interesting. And here we are, which is just as well, if you don't want to hear more about St. Paul!'

'No, thanks,' Keith said fervently, and gave an involuntary smile as Rowena chuckled at his shying away from the subject. 'It looks like quite a crowd today. Henderson was once an army chaplain, so he should know what he's talking about.'

Groups of people were chatting informally all over the room, and Rowena went to speak to a science teacher she knew. Miss Maxton was studying a list of names in a notebook, and she greeted Rowena with joy.

'Oh, thank goodness you're home again! You're the best organiser we've ever had, and I want you on a sub-committee right now. It's about this African business—'

Rowena shook her head. 'I'm sorry, Miss Maxton, I think we'd be on opposite sides. The British didn't

166

move in until the legal government asked for their help, and it's the rebels who started the bloodshed and who are now yelling about it to the United Nations.'

'But haven't you *heard* about the weapons the soldiers are using? They – they're appalling! It's got to be stopped before the conflagration spreads!'

'Isn't that what the British are trying to do?' Rowena asked. 'They and the legal government have offered the most generous terms for cease-fire talks, and this is one instance where the rebels are savages financed from outside, and not giving a damn about their own country.'

The expressions of those in the group, which now included Keith, were of uncertainty and incomprehension, so Rowena just smiled at Miss Maxton and turned away.

'You won't go on the committee?' Keith asked, as they sat at one end of the front row of chairs. 'Miss Maxton was depending on your help, because you seem to have more free time than any of us, and you've done that kind of thing so often before.'

'With more reason, I hope,' Rowena said crisply. 'Show some people a weapon these days, and they set up a howl without caring who's wielding it, or which bloodstained rebel they're supporting. I wonder where Mr. Henderson stands on this question?'

'I don't know,' Keith told her, frowning, and she studied the clergyman who was taking his place on the dais. He sat at one end of the table and smiled round at the company, a good-looking man of middle-age in dark clerical robes. He had become Chairman while Rowena was away, and this was the first time she had heard or seen him at close quarters. The subject of his address was the organisation of protest and demonstration, and his experience of the right and wrong ways to go about them. He had a fine sense of humour, he spoke well, and the intense silence in the hall was a tribute to the interest he was arousing.

He had taken part in an anti-nuclear demonstration in Paris the previous week, and his features softened as he recalled it. 'It was a quiet, solemn march,' he said, 'and all the more effective for that. Our banners told our message, and we felt as if Christ were walking with us. In fact, if He were still on this earth, He would have joined us.'

'Oh, no!' Rowena exclaimed, and because she was in the front row, Mr. Henderson heard her, and hesitated.

'I'm so sorry,' Rowena murmured, scarlet to her hairline. 'I didn't mean to interrupt.'

He smiled down at her. 'But I'm interested. You sounded quite shocked! I really would like to know why.'

Rowena took a deep breath. 'All right. It struck me as blasphemy, and then as sheer vanity. Christ wasn't a – a meek, silent person when evil was directed at something outside Himself. He made a whip of small cords, and *drove* the tradesmen from the temple of God, and He *overthrew* the tables of the money-changers. He even told us that He came not to bring peace, but a sword.'

'Ah,' Mr. Henderson said, 'you may be confusing the meaning of the word "peace." In the Old Testament translation, it means "welfare" and is external. In the New Testament, the sense is of "heart peace," and it is internal.'

Rowena frowned in thought. 'Then why do we in this organisation use it so much as the kind of earthly peace which is the opposite of war? It's dishonest.'

'*Do* be quiet,' Keith muttered in an agony of embarrassment, but Rowena barely heard him.

'I think this is a private argument we'll have to pursue later,' Mr. Henderson said with relish, but his eyes were thoughtful as Rowena looked right back at him and waited for him to go on.

At the end of his talk, he invited questions, and with

168

some idea of retrieving lost ground, Keith asked him if it was his Army service which had set him on the pacifist path. Mr. Henderson admitted that it was, that he had joined as a chaplain to bring his services to the fighting men, that he had found no glory and no gain in war, and that it had all been horror and grief and waste.

'It was all so futile,' he said slowly, 'that it didn't seem possible that mankind could ever do it again. I was so *sure* then that the world must live at peace when it was all over.'

'I know,' Rowena said with sympathy. 'It's beyond belief that we could be on the brink again. But – who did you hope to be rid of when the war was over? The children of light, or the children of darkness?'

'*Rid* of?' he echoed, and Rowena nodded.

'Well, the Bible calls them the children of God and the children of the devil, and they'll both be around right up till the end of time. They'll never compromise, so we'll always have wars and rumours of wars in this world.' She stared ahead, her eyes blank with thought. 'That's it – that's what I've been trying to get hold of – "iniquity shall abound, but he that shall endure to the end, the same shall be saved." We are asked to – to *endure*, and not merely to accept and give in.'

There were about forty people grouped round the dais, some of them considering the subject with interest, and others, like Keith, obviously finding the turn of the discussion distasteful.

'I respect the deep thought you've given to this,' Mr. Henderson said after a moment, 'but we can so often take texts of Scripture and mould them to our own views. You can't "live peaceably with all men" if you're so determined to fight them.'

Rowena smiled at him with some regret. 'I prefer "resist" to "fight," and you haven't quoted the other half of that same text. St. Paul said: "Live peaceably with all men, *as much as lieth in you*." No one understood human nature better than he did, and he knew it wasn't possible for an imperfect man to live at peace all the time.'

'Are you a member of this organisation?' he asked curiously. 'Forgive me for asking, but I haven't seen you before, and you certainly don't sound like one of us!'

Rowena thought back and sighed a little. 'I've been a member for five years, I've gone on marches, attended demonstrations, and been arrested. But I'm afraid I'm now arguing myself out of all sympathy with the movement as it is at present. We seem to have become self-righteous, seeing ourselves as the conscience of the world, and assuming that the people who won't join us are either warmongers or those who don't care that the world is on the way to destruction. And that's a terrible, proud, narrow-minded assumption to make.'

'She spent three months in Yugoslavia,' Keith said bitterly, 'and she came back a partisan brigand.'

'Ah,' Mr. Henderson said with understanding, and it was in his eyes that he knew of the martyrdom of the Serbs. 'But that Government are looking forward instead of back, and they protest strongly at what they call imperialist aggression in all parts of the world.'

'I can love the people without agreeing with the Government,' Rowena said cheerfully. 'These phrases are merely doctrinaire slogans, the outward and visible signs of being good Communists! But I'll tell you this – they'll never bow their heads before brutal aggressors like the Nazis were. They recognised evil for what it was, and they resisted it to the death, and they'll do it again if the need ever arises.'

Miss Maxton stood up and glared at Rowena before turning to the Chairman. 'Could we change the subject, please? This is *not* a Debating Society! The mere possibility of another war is the evil which must be recognised, and we are pledged to do all in our power to see that it never happens. Could we now go on to discuss plans for the rally in Hyde Park next week?'

Rowena gave her an apologetic look, but it was lost on Miss Maxton and on most of the others. So she sat back and took no further part in the meeting, her thoughts far away, and a lightness at the back of her mind as if she had lost the anxiety which had been growing heavier for a long time. For five years she had been groping through the emotional mists of fear and hatred of a sudden end to the world, and now she had come out on the other side of the fog, and found that it had all led to acceptance of life as it must be. Not to acceptance of wrongs which could be righted, or of ills which could be aided, but to the acceptance of man's imperfect humanity, his preference for 'darkness rather than light,' and to the necessity to take a stand for truth against error. The danger was that you had to be so sure which was which, and for that you could only rely on instinct, and knowledge, and guidance.

She was still in a deep reverie when the bustle in the hall indicated that the meeting was over. Keith was talking to the man on his other side, and when Rowena stood up, Mr. Henderson came over to her.

'I'd like to have met you on a television panel,' he said as he shook hands. 'It isn't often that anyone meets me on my own ground, so to speak!'

'A lot of it was fortuitous,' Rowena admitted. 'Three people turned my thoughts towards Scripture recently, and I've been attending a course on St. Paul. But I must have been led, because what it has done for me is clear up a lot of the problems that arose from too little knowledge of the world and of human nature. I know very little now, but at least it's a beginning.'

'And you're definitely leaving us?'

She glanced round, noting that Keith had joined them, and that Miss Maxton was hovering nearby. 'Yes, I must. I hope you all succeed in your aims, I hope that very much, but this kind of association is too – too nebulous for me. I have to learn to use my own judgment, to reason things out, to rely on my own morals and standards, to set up my own values.'

'You think we don't do that?'

'Not as a body anyway, because I can only look back on five lost years as far as my work here has been concerned. I thought our conformity and our youth and our common aim were wonderful, but they were the values of the – the herd, and they weren't of my own reasoning. The Hitler Youth had conformity and a common aim too, and I'm sure they found it wonderful, but in their enthusiasm for the movement, they lost sight of where it must lead them.'

This was heresy of the blackest, and although Mr. Henderson had an understanding twinkle in his eye, Miss Maxton looked poleaxed, and Keith gripped Rowena's arm and walked out with her after the briefest of farewells to the others.

It was a cool, clear evening, and Rowena belted her white wool coat and looked up with pleasure at the silent Saturday buildings of the City of London. She was content to let Keith take as long as he liked over his choice of words, and she hoped that this time they would really reflect what was in his mind. How sad that it didn't matter any more.

'That was quite an exhibition,' he said at last, as they walked along the street. 'I only hope you didn't set out beforehand with the intention of pinning the new Chairman to the wall?'

Rowena sighed. 'It never entered my head, until he talked about Christ marching with the demonstrators. I

172

am sorry if I embarrassed you, but at least you know I'll never be there again.'

'But why?' he burst out. 'Why have you changed so much? You were the liveliest member of the organisation when I first knew you!'

'You heard all my reasons when I gave them to Mr. Henderson. Didn't you believe them?'

He made an impatient noise like a snort. 'All that talk about morals and the Hitler Youth and the sainted Paul? You *enjoyed* it all for the sake of arguments that made you sound clever, if they had meant anything!'

'I admit to enjoying the debate, and that was wicked of me, but I'm not a saint like Paul! Anyway, I meant every word, however it sounded to you, and I can't explain any more than I've done already. I think we'd better take a taxi – Mrs. Waring was staying on to let your mother in, but she'll be all alone by now. There isn't much more to say, about us, I mean.'

'Us?' he echoed, standing still, and she looked up at him, sorry for his startled expression as he realised that he had been speaking his mind at last. He would have to admit, now, that this was a fundamental cleavage and not a mere lover's quarrel.

'Oh, devil take it,' he said unhappily. 'You're making it sound worse than the problem of a Jew marrying a Roman Catholic! One of them must give way, but this is – is just a division of interests. We could agree to disagree about pacifism!'

'It made you mad today, though,' Rowena said. 'Odd how that subject of all under the sun can raise such passions for and against! Come on, there's a taxi.'

Keith sat in deep thought until they reached Pimlico, and Rowena left him to it. Mrs. Manning was contentedly waiting in the drawing-room, sipping the sherry which had been brought to her by Mrs. Waring. Keith went upstairs,

173

and his mother complimented Rowena on the lampshades which were new since her last visit. Rowena felt guilty that Mrs. Manning had had no warning at all of the impending break-up of the engagement, and her dismay increased when the older woman searched in her handbag and handed over a visiting card.

'Such nice engraving, dear, don't you think?' she asked. 'Keith had them done ages ago, but of course he hasn't used any of them yet. I wanted him to have "Belgravia" under the street name, but he said it wasn't usual.'

'No,' Rowena agreed faintly, staring at the engraved 'Keith Manning' over her own address. 'We're really Pimlico, although we're on the border, and both districts are S.W.1. Perhaps we – we'd better not tell him I've seen this – if it's to be a surprise—'

Mrs. Manning gave the card a complacent glance and replaced it in her bag. 'I'm sure he'll have some done for you too, dear, if you would like them. Have you any news of your great-uncle? It's such a pity not to be able to make plans.'

'No, I haven't heard,' Rowena said. 'I – excuse me – I must have a look at the dinner.'

She fled to the kitchen, irritated by the ill fortune which had made Mrs. Manning one of the party. Of course, she hadn't known that the afternoon's meeting would bring everything to a head, but it wasn't to be thought of that Mrs. Manning should spread the evening twittering about the wedding preparations. There was no chance to say anything to Keith before dinner, as he didn't appear until they were going into the dining-room, and Rowena wondered if he were deliberately using his mother as a buffer. Conversation was somewhat strained during the meal, but Mrs. Manning never noticed because she was absorbed in the wedgwood-blue and white elegance of the room. Rowena knew she was thrilled into a trance at the

174

thought that the house was no longer Anne's. It belonged to Rowena, the woman her son was to marry, and therefore it was going to belong to Keith too, and soon no one would recall that he hadn't been the master from the beginning.

Rowena shrugged mentally, with faint distaste. It wasn't her fault that Mrs. Manning was willing to put up with any girl who could give her son a background like this, and any disappointment would be all for the loss of the house and not of the wife.

Keith put dishes through the kitchen hatch, but when he didn't follow to help with the coffee, Rowena knew that he was evading being alone with her for the time being. Well, he would have to face up to it sooner or later, and it must be tonight. As she wheeled the trolley across the hall to the drawing-room, Rowena saw the corner of an envelope under Mrs. Manning's hat and gloves on the table. Trust that selfish woman to place her belongings over the mail which had been left there.

There were three letters, and when she saw that one was from Anne, Rowena hurried into the drawing-room and asked Keith to pour the coffee. 'Excuse me,' she said as she slit the envelope. 'The post arrived after I left this morning, and I didn't see it on the hall table when I came in.

'Glory be!' she exclaimed after a moment, her eyes wide. 'Mother's expecting a baby – round about Christmas, she says – she hopes it will be a boy for Viktor!'

She gazed across the room, frantic thoughts chasing each other in her mind. Mother would be forty-one . . . would it mean a hospital, or were the local doctors enough? . . . there wouldn't be many guests at Christmas, if any . . . oh, she *had* to be there to help . . . only, they hadn't said they needed or wanted her . . . would Simon and Natalya have moved into the Nimani house by then? . . . for herself, there was always Marija's little place at Izvor . . .

175

She had been looking at Keith and his mother without really seeing them, and now she became aware that their reaction to the news had been varying degrees of shock, distaste, and dismay. She hadn't said anything herself, and her abstraction must have seemed like the same kind of shock the Mannings had had.

'Such a pity,' Mrs. Manning regretted, and she looked at her adored son as if picturing the arrival of a new brother or sister then. 'Oh dear, I just can't imagine it! *Such* a gap – how old are you, Rowena, dear?'

'Twenty-two by then,' Rowena said with some inner amusement. 'Mother will only be forty-one, she looks a lot younger, and her health has always been wonderful.'

'At least we won't have to cope with a half-brother or sister over here,' Keith said thoughtfully. 'I certainly won't shout it around that we've got one who's twenty-two years younger than I am! We might have guessed this could happen, of course. It just seems – well, odd.'

'It would, to you,' Rowena said, and Keith's jaw slackened as he met the hard, bright sparkle in her eyes. 'They're in love, so why shouldn't they have babies? I hope they have as many more as they want. I think it's wonderful, and I'm thrilled to bits.'

'You didn't look it!' Keith back-tracked hurriedly. 'I mean – well, it was a shock to us all, but if you're quite pleased, there's no more to be said.'

'I'm afraid there is,' she said in quiet, even tones. 'What about this afternoon? We don't meet on common ground anywhere at all.'

'I've decided to resign too,' he told her. 'One of us has to give in, so I will. There won't be any more friction. It's mad to let politics and religion come between two people in love.'

'Oh, Keith,' she said sadly, 'you don't believe a word of that! You were simply furious with me today, and it

176

would happen again, lots of times. You can't silence your conscience, even for love. And – it's not love, is it? You know that, and you've known it for weeks.'

He stared at her, red tinging his cheekbones, and then pressed his startled mother back in her chair as he took a few steps back and fore in front of the mantelpiece.

'If *only* you hadn't stayed on in that beastly country,' he said bitterly. 'I knew all the time it was a mistake to allow it, but I took a chance, and this is the thanks I get!'

'To *allow* it? But why didn't you say what you thought? I was so grateful for your lovely letters that they were like a millstone round my neck! Why did you bother?'

He shrugged. 'I suppose so that gratitude would bring you back, if nothing else would. You mentioned common ground just now – we had an awful lot before we ever decided to go to Yugoslavia. I just wanted to hold on to what we had.'

'But it was never enough,' Rowena murmured, 'and as soon as I got back we both knew it. You've worked terribly hard to patch over the cracks, and there was nothing that was between us that was worth all that hard labour.'

Mrs. Manning had finally gathered that her son and his fiancée were on the verge of parting, and the shock was considerable. 'You can't – you mustn't!' she stammered. 'Everything is fixed – you're going to live here together!'

'I'm afraid not,' Rowena said, and intercepted the impatient, warning glance which Keith cast at his mother. So her original suspicions had been right after all. Almost any crack was worth patching over, any personable girl worth having, if a Georgian gem of a house in a fashionable part of London went with her. She mustn't be upset, even by honest criticism, in case the future was jeopardised, and the image of a man dreaming over her perfume was more seemly than the truth that he had spent hours pretending to be the master of the house while she was away. He was prepared to strangle his deepest convictions because she no longer agreed with them, but he *must* have known that there would come a reckoning, because he was basically honest in his beliefs, and he couldn't have denied them for long. But by that time, he would have been the man in possession, and it seemed that all he wanted was to be able to hold on until then, even if it meant the temporary surrender of pride and honesty and truth.

'What are you going to do?' Keith asked, prompted by curiosity, because there was tired hopelessness about him which told that he had given up the struggle.

'I – I'd like to go out to Mother about November, but she hasn't said she'd like me to go. After the New Year – I don't know – come back here and get a job maybe.'

Keith smiled faintly, his first that evening. 'I doubt it. You'll stay in Yugoslavia for the rest of your life, perhaps not at Srebro Kara, but up among the mountains of Montenegro. You'll take the donkey the old woman gave you, and you may even wear homespun, and you'll take long, cool looks at all the tourists and be glad you're not one of them.'

'I think you may be among the prophets,' Rowena said, surprised that he understood her dreams so well. But then, he always had, and had been determined to change them.

'This house,' Mrs. Manning said eagerly. 'You can't leave it empty with just Mrs. Waring popping in every day. You'll have to let it, and it's best to have tenants you know—'

'Mother,' Keith said with weary patience as he drew her to her feet. 'That will do. Rowena will sell this house, and she will get at least thirty thousand pounds for it. She's going to be a peasant in the wilds, and not an absentee landlord.'

Rowena ran upstairs for her ring box while the other two were putting on their coats, and when Mrs. Manning had stalked silently out to the front steps, she gave the box to Keith.

'I'm sorry,' she said quietly. 'I really am. But we both know it would never have worked out.'

'No, I suppose it wouldn't. I'm sorry too.'

When she had closed the door behind them, she realised that now there were very few people in London who were likely to come calling. Her interests had been so bound up in the peace movement that she had made no close friends outside it, and her school and college friends were scattered all over the world.

That didn't matter for a few days. She had written to her mother, telling her that she would like to come to Srebro Kara in a couple of months, and asking if there were any particular possessions she would like to have brought out. She also asked if Anne had any objections to the thought of selling the house some day, and she made tentative enquiries about the tenancy of Marija's little house. It was only after the letter was gone that Rowena remembered that she hadn't mentioned Keith or the breaking of the engagement. Not that it mattered. They would all know that Keith was out of her life when she was considering a return to the country so soon.

She expected a cable, or at least an air mail answer by return, but ten days went by and she was still prowling round the house and mentally tagging articles and furniture that might be taken or left behind. Some of the excitement engendered by Anne's news had faded, and there was time to look ahead more clearly and to wonder how she would cope with seeing Simon every day. Now that Anne was expecting a baby, Natalya's services as cook and housekeeper would be more vital than ever.

Rowena thought about that when she was in bed one

night, and she stared into the darkness, remembering Natalya's wistful hope that Anne would gradually take over from her, so that she could marry Simon and start a family. Now that that hope was knocked on the head, it would be – funny if Anne's daughter should come along in the nick of time to enable the marriage to go ahead after all. As Natalya had said, all they had ever waited for was someone to take her place, so that Viktor wouldn't be left in the lurch after having been so good to her people.

Rowena turned restlessly, oppressed by the silence and emptiness of the house, certain, in the small hours of lowered vitality, that she would never have the strength to even look at Simon without wanting him. If loving him from a thousand miles away was a sharp, despairing ache, how could she bear being near him when he belonged to another woman?

The following day, she went out when Mrs. Waring left, merely because she didn't want to be alone in the house. She had waited for the second post, and when there was nothing from her mother she felt like bursting into tears. *Why* should it take them so long to decide if they wanted her with them or not? She had been so sure of her welcome before, but she was only beginning to realise that however much he might love an adopted daughter, Viktor's own child must be a much more thrilling part of his life.

It was dusk when she returned slowly homewards, and she bit her lip when she saw lights going on in almost every house but her own. These houses were well-built and almost soundproof, and the thought of another evening and night spent in solitary doubt was appalling. If Mother would even tell her not to come until the summer, she would know what she was supposed to be doing, and she would be able to settle to something else. She hesitated, wondering about dining out and going to the cinema, and about six doors ahead of her, she saw a man looking closely at the number on each house.

It wasn't possible . . . and yet, that tall, lean figure . . . the shape of the dark head . . . and he was carrying a holdall, and he wasn't sure of his whereabouts . . .

'Simon,' she whispered, and started running, still not certain, and terrified that she might be wrong after all.

He looked up at the sound of running footsteps, stood rigid for a second, and then dropped the bag and held out his arms. She threw herself against him, shaking, clutching at his coat as if to make sure she was touching him and not dreaming it all and, as he had done before, he held her with tender strength and found her lips with his own.

'It is all right,' Simon said at last, holding her a little away from him and smiling down at her. 'But perhaps we should go inside before your neighbours become interested!'

'Yes,' Rowena managed, and gripped his hand with such fear that he stopped after lifting his bag, and looked at her with concern.

'I have come for you,' he said quietly. 'You are going home with me, and nothing will prevent that, and I shall never let you go as long as I live. Do you understand that?'

'Yes – oh yes, please – take me home with you, and never, never let me go!'

She pulled him up the steps and opened the door, and after she had switched on the lights in the drawing-room, she stood by the curtains she had just drawn as if she were afraid to turn round.

'I am still here,' Simon said gently, and lifted her into his arms and sat on the couch with her. 'Now you will tell me why you did not come back to me when it seems that you love me as I love you. And why you wrote foolishness about living in Marija's house. We guessed from your letter that you had parted from Keith, so why do you look at me even now as if it cannot be true that you are here in my arms?'

She gazed into his dark brown eyes, and touched his cheek with loving fingers. 'But I was waiting for news of your marriage to Natalya! You said yourself on the day I left that neither of us was free!'

'I did? I could only have meant that we were not free because you were engaged to Keith, and because you had told us not long before you left that your heart was where your treasure was, and that that was here in London. And what is this about marrying Natalya? I have never even kissed her on her birthday! It is more possible that I would consider marrying Marija!'

'Oh, no,' Rowena said in a low, stricken voice. 'She *couldn't* have been lying all the time! She first told me you were both longing to get married about a week after I got there! She asked me to keep it quiet, because you didn't want to let Viktor down during his first season – she said you both wanted a big family, and that she couldn't be housekeeper at Srebro Kara, and the mother of your children as well! And on the morning I left, she warned me off. She begged me not to take what belonged to her! She knew very well that I was in love with you then.'

Rowena had been proud of her progress in Serbo-Croatian, but Simon's rapid and furious expletives were beyond her. He calmed down after a while, asked her for the rest of the story, and when she had finished, she kissed him and went to get Natalya's post card which said that the move to the Nimani house was a beginning.

'It is no wonder that she walked out on us on the day your letter arrived,' Simon said grimly. 'Anne was so excited that she was laughing and crying at the same time, and when she read your letter to us, the first thing we realised was that you must have broken with Keith. We could not understand your desire to live in Izvor which you had never even seen, but at that moment, I decided to come and get you. I had no up-to-date passport or papers, and that is why I was not here days ago.'

'But what could Natalya have hoped to gain? She must have known that I would find out some day that you hadn't been engaged all these months.'

'And by then you would be safely married to Keith, and all "danger" from you would be over. She knew I was in love with you – she teased me about it on the day Keith left, when you came to stay at Srebro Kara. You look surprised! Had you not guessed all along that I adored you?'

She laid her cheek against his, and closed her eyes. 'Heavens, no,' she whispered. 'How could I have gone away as I did if I had known you loved me too? Why didn't you *make* me understand?'

'Oh, darling,' Simon said with a small, regretful laugh, 'you sounded so convincing when you spoke of loving and marrying Keith! You loved my country, but you were prepared to stay away from it because the man you were to marry had a dislike for it! I had some very faint hopes that some day you might care for me – until you looked so radiant as you said that your heart was here where your treasure was.'

'I – I couldn't grovel in front of you all,' Rowena said, 'and I had no idea that Natalya wasn't *your* treasure then. Darling, darling, isn't it terrible what pride can do to our lives!'

'We will have no more of it on either side,' he said soberly. 'We have had an escape which will haunt me for the rest of my life. If you had married Keith, perhaps I would have become so lonely that marriage with Natalya would have seemed a solution. There was no one else, and on the surface she had many good points, although there was not much to her mind or her heart. She is a primitive,

183

and she did not love me for myself, but only for my prospects. Yes, she might have won after all, but now she is gone, and Ivanca Nimini is a better cook than she ever was.'

'Why have you taken a house of your own?'

'Oh – just to be alone sometimes, to have my own books and possessions around me, to think about you! I did not intend to sleep there every night – just when it suited me to do so. This house of yours is very beautiful, as much as I have seen of it. What will you think of living in mine?'

'That I'm luckier than I ever deserved,' Rowena said blissfully. 'If you were with me, I'd be quite happy in the stall that Uncle Oliver built for Petak and Djordje! Where *is* he anyway?'

Simon grinned. 'I almost forgot! Please, is it safe for him to return to England now? When he knew you would not marry Keith until he had returned to give you away, he said that nothing would bring him until you changed your mind! He was so sure you would change in the end, but the rest of us were not so sure. Your letters were so cheerful that it was disgusting! Yes, I know, that was your pride again. I have also to tell you that Ivan Mitrev made a special journey to tell us that you were already half-dead with homesickness when you went ashore at Trieste. He told us of the little sailors falling asleep in your lap and round your neck, and when he demanded that we send for you at once, he was *so* delighted that I was on the point of leaving to fetch you.'

'Dear Ivan,' Rowena said softly. 'I loved him, and all those boys who were as homesick as I was. Now I'll get some supper for us. You must be starving, and I'm hungry for the first time in weeks!'

'I will have to find somewhere to stay—'

'No! I'm not letting you out of my sight! Please, Simon, don't leave me again!'